CIRCLE THE SOUL SOFTLY

CIRCLE THE SOUL SOFTLY

DAVIDA WILLS HURWIN

HarperCollins*Publishers*

Library of Congress Cataloging-in-Publication Data
Hurwin, Davida, 1950-
Circle the soul softly / Davida Wills Hurwin.— 1st ed.
p.   cm.
Summary: Suppressed memories of childhood sexual abuse resurface, jeopardizing
fifteen-year-old Kate's relationship with her new boyfriend.
ISBN-10: 0-06-077505-X (trade bdg.) — ISBN-13: 978-0-06-077505-6 (trade bdg.)
ISBN-10: 0-06-077506-8 (lib. bdg.) — ISBN-13: 978-0-06-077506-3 (lib. bdg.)
[1. Self-perception—Fiction. 2. Child sexual abuse—Fiction.
3. Incest—Fiction. 4. Post-traumatic stress disorder—Fiction.] I. Title.
PZ7.H95735Cir 2006   2005005714
[Fic]—dc22   CIP
AC

Typography by Sara Rabinowitz
1 2 3 4 5 6 7 8 9 10

First Edition

For Margie

Thank You
Kaitlyn, Amanda, and Andrew
Ms. Virginia Russell and Ms. Colleen Bright Ross
Maria Modugno and HarperCollins
Bonnie Nadell

Gene Marc and Frazier Malone Hurwin

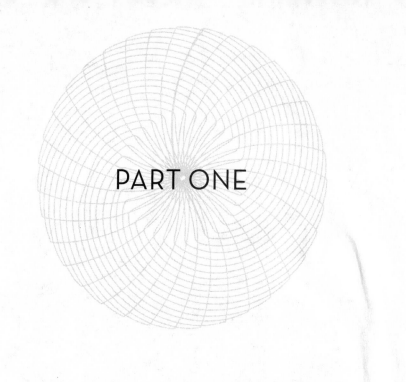

PART ONE

ONE

Michael takes the U-turn *after* the light clicks to red, screeching the tires and almost hitting some old woman in a jeep. He flips her off, leans over, and shows me his Dumb Jock face. We screech again as we almost miss the second turn. Every single person in every single car in the carpool line glares. I scrunch down in the seat and remember why I hate my brother.

"This is *it?*"

Michael has stopped in the middle of the street. Now everyone on the sidewalk is staring too.

"Move the car, butthead."

"Do you know how much this place costs?"

"What do you care—you're not paying." *Just breathe, Katie, breathe.* Finally he moves, drives, parks. This is definitely not how I visualized my first day at a new school.

"Skates, are you sure you want to go here?"

"Do *not* call me 'Skates.'" I grab my schedule and get out. If it wouldn't get more stares, I'd slam the door.

"Let me walk you. I want to see the rich kids."

"Hey—better idea—go die somewhere, okay?"

★ ★ ★

First I run into a bench. No big deal, no one's watching. Then I go into the wrong room, with the twelfth-grade students instead of tenth. I get stuck between an Eminem look-alike and a troupe of blank-faced, black-haired maybe-females with extreme makeup. From the other side of the room, two anorexic *Vogue* model types check me out. The redhead whispers something and the blonde starts laughing, quietly, behind her hand. Eminem sneers down at me and nods once, like I care. I put them all on my list of those needing paper cuts. Then the blonde rolls her eyes and I smile.

I smile!

I miss the tenth-grade orientation talk completely, so I follow the crowd. I stand in line, get my picture taken, and follow another crowd down the alley to stand in line again. I'm paired with a fairly normal-looking girl who immediately assures me she thinks *I'm* just fine but practically every other girl in our grade is a bitch. We get our books and stand in still another line to pay for them.

I fumble for my mom's credit card and bang into the edge of a table. My plastic bags split at the seams and three million books clatter to the floor. In the nanosecond of silence that follows, someone says: "Omigod, I will never get out of here." The whole room laughs; I am publicly revealed: Attention everyone! Stupid Kate is here—can't you see her *smiling*?

How I get from the book-buying place to Michael's car is not entirely clear. Of course, he's standing outside it, tall, lanky, serene, *fitting right in*. I hate him. The blonde and the redhead from twelfth grade drive by us in a little black BMW. They glance over and the redhead winks. He tips his head in their direction and the blonde almost smiles. I do not even exist. I hate him even more.

4

★ ★ ★

Here's the list:

I run into benches and walls and other random objects, I don't *understand* the social thing, I always think people are dissing me, and the only person I'm *able* to get pissed at is my brother—but only if no one's looking.

And—my personal favorite—*I smile.* Constantly. It doesn't matter how stupid, angry, depressed, or embarrassed I am—I still smile. The only time I actually *don't* smile is when I'm doing a part in a play. Oh, but wait—that isn't real life, is it?

This morning was supposed to mark the official birth of my new identity—the person who can cope with anything. New house, new father—well, sort of—new school, *new girl.* This one is funny and knows what to say. She has a best friend and they make plans every weekend. She gets IMed the second she goes online. She doesn't space out during daylight and has regular dreams, not scary nightmares. She never bumps into stuff and she has an extremely cool, extremely individual way of dressing. Her boyfriend? One of the cutest guys at school.

I swear she's in here.

I just don't know how to get her out.

So—I walk. It helps me think. Or *not*, depending on the day. It moves me forward, anyway, especially when Stupid Kate has appeared. I don't have to talk to people, not even my mom. I just say I'm exploring my new neighborhood.

It's weird. Brentwood is one of the most expensive places in California, and it reminds me of Santa Rosa, which definitely is not. Willow trees along the streets, their branches arching almost to the center. Sunlight peeking through. Breezes painting shadow dancers on the sidewalk. I like being here. Of course, in Santa Rosa, there'd be leaves rustling now, crunching under my feet. I miss that. But in Santa Rosa, I'd also have that eerie feeling that someone was following me, and I'd stop every so often to see if I could catch the sound of them in the leaves.

Here, in my new Normal and Connected Life, the leaves have been sent who knows where by loud little cleaning machines. And even with no one around—no gardeners, pets, children, not even cars going by—I will not have that feeling because I will not allow it.

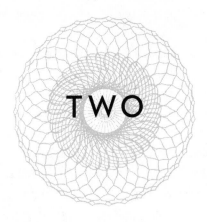

TWO

"Goddammit!" a girl shouts. I look up to see her jump out of the way of the black BMW from yesterday. It's the first full-length day of school, and I'm sitting on the benches in the alley in front of the little black-box theater, waiting for first period to start, feeling conspicuous and invisible at the same time.

A dark, smiling boy sticks his head out the passenger side of the car. "It's a car, Heather . . . *car*? Maybe you could move out of the way?"

"Maybe Stacey could learn to drive?" Heather's jeans are very low and way too tight and quite a significant roll of pink flesh bulges out between them and her tank top. It's twelve degrees and she has no jacket, but neither do most of the other kids. Maybe the rich are immune to the morning cold?

Stacey smiles a deadly smile and holds up her middle finger. Heather holds up *her* finger as Stacey parks directly in front of where I'm sitting. I recognize Stacey as the redhead *Vogue* model who liked me so much at orientation. I negotiate with the Universe to allow me to melt into the ground, but as usual, it's not listening. Stacey, Dark Smiling Boy, and Movie Star Blonde emerge like royalty from their car and I drop my head, pretending to read.

I need not have worried. Unworthy of their attention, I blend with my surroundings and they slide right by. The first bell rings. Hunched over and praying for continued invisibility, I skulk without incident past the library. Alas, I relax my guard to check my schedule and map and don't realize Stacey and Movie Star Blonde have stopped a few steps in front of me. Of course, I bump into them. I step on the Blonde's foot, knock her backward, send her books flying and basically drop her into a planter. A pause in the morning ripples out from where I'm standing.

"Shit!" says the Blonde.

"Layla?" Stacey asks, extending her hand. "Omigod, are you okay?"

I am now a large, wordless lump. In some still-functioning part of my brain, I wonder who would name their child "Layla."

"You oughta watch where you're going," Stacey hisses, checking me out and finding me even uglier than I feel.

"Why did she hit *me*?" Layla whines. "Why can't anybody ever hit *you*? Why does it always have to be me?" This makes Stacey giggle.

By the time I manage to whisper, "I am so sorry," the Movie Stars have left the building. Dark Smiling Boy has turned into Laughing Butthead Boy. I blink a couple times and my legs finally work, but I can feel the edges of my vision filling in. I duck around a corner into a hallway. It's ninth grade all over again. How did this happen so soon?

It's always the same. I'm in the hallway and the Monster appears. I start to run, knowing if I can reach the door, I'll be safe, but the walls close in and the hallway stretches, like in a cartoon, and the more I run, the bigger the Monster gets. I can't see its face but I hear it breathing, sucking up the air, and I want to scream but I can't catch my breath and now the hallway's forever and the door has disappeared and I feel claws picking me up and I know the minute I see the Monster's face I'll die—and then there's a flash, like sunlight, and it's Minnie Mouse in her yellow polka dot dress, and . . .

I wake up.

THREE

"Acting is something you do for an audience," Tess explains, "which is why my auditions are never private."

Tess is the incredibly awesome drama teacher who's way older than my mom, dresses like one of the kids, and gets absolute respect from everybody. She has long, dark hair with gray strands throughout and today is wearing tight black jeans and a long-sleeved T-shirt. She looks pointedly at Laughing Butthead Boy, who immediately bows his head, no doubt to hide a grin. Layla pokes him and Stacey shows us the other side of her perfect face. In Santa Rosa, theater kids are the ones who don't fit anyplace else. Here in LA, everyone's actor, unless they're a director. And everyone is beautiful. For my third strike, I expect I'll find out they're also talented.

Tess is collecting audition cards; she smiles and holds out her hand for mine. "How am I going to know how you carry yourself in front of people if you audition just for me?" she asks, and even though I know she's not really talking to me, I nod.

Butthead Boy is staring. We've been in the room twenty minutes and he is just now noticing me. "Who's that?" he whispers, and the *Vogue* Twins peek over. If my heart pounds any harder, the girl sitting next to me will hear it.

"Who cares?" Stacey answers, dismissing me with a shrug. I can't remember one line of my audition monologue.

"I think she's hot," he says. Sweat is flowing down the insides of my arms.

Layla pokes his shoulder. "She's twelve, you moron. Leave her alone." I don't know if she meant me to hear that, but it's obvious I did from the color flushing into my cheeks. Not one of them recognizes me from yesterday.

"Okay, babies, here we go." Tess looks down at our index cards. "The order's by chance—I shuffled everybody, and there you are." She reads the first one. "Kaitlyn O'Connor."

My hands start to shake.

"You want someone to work with?" Tess asks, smiling, but all business now. I stare a second, process what she's asked me, then nod. "Boy or girl?"

"Boy, please."

"Jake, onstage." Butthead Boy stands up.

This is a bad movie and cannot be happening in real life. There are at least a dozen other boys in the room and none of them have the *Vogue* Twins attached. I can see Jake trying to pretend he wants to do this. I pray for an earthquake.

"Name of the play?" Tess asks.

I make myself speak. "*Echoes.* By Richard Nash. Where Tilda tells Sam about The Person."

I start to prepare. Jake rolls his eyes. He tries to hide it, but I always see what I'm not supposed to—like Stacey-Layla studiously *not* reacting. And the girl who was sitting next to me, giving them a dirty look, confirming their importance. Stupid Kate appears, but I have no time for her.

"Now listen to me, Sammy. Don't you see what the technique is?"

Jake blinks twice, fast. Everyone else slips out of my head. There's only Tilda now, and she has something to tell Sam. He doesn't want to hear it; I have to find a way to make him listen. Jake's face changes as I pull him in. But I don't care anymore what "Jake" thinks—he's merely Sam, reacting to my words. The monologue zooms by.

" . . . and don't you tell me how Goddamn beautiful life is until you tell me why we die! And if you say everything has a purpose in the world—*what is the use of pain*?!"

Jake morphs back to Butthead Boy. I blink and slip back to Katie. Tess is smiling. The other kids are looking and for the first time it feels like they're actually *seeing* me. They clap their hands. All of them, even Jake. Only Stacey ignores me. She's busy in her backpack.

"Well," Tess says, "that worked. Let me see your hair pulled back. Okay, good, that makes you look much older. I want you to read for Maggie and Agnes. Sides are on the table in the greenroom. Callbacks are next week." She winks at me then looks back down at her cards. "All right. Next victim . . ."

FOUR

I couldn't have been much more than two. I don't know where exactly we were, how we got there, or who else was with us. I do remember the sand. I'd never seen so much of it, and I loved how my bare feet slapped down as we walked toward the water. I turned my head from side to side to catch the icy drops of fog in the air.

I remember holding his hand—reaching straight up to grab it. The low roar of the waves and the salty spray on my face were simply glorious; I delighted in the way my laughter disappeared into the sky without even being heard. The gray of the sky melted into the horizon and the fog closed off the land behind us, so the whole world was only me and my daddy and the ocean crashing toward us. The pit of my stomach churned and my skin tingled with anticipation. He had to yell to be heard over the water. "Hold on, Kates, here it comes!"

The wave must have broken yards in front of us because the water barely covered my ankles. I gasped at the cold then laughed out loud again, clinging even tighter to my daddy's hand. He was laughing too, I remember the tone of it—low and full and mine.

But as the ocean retreated and stole the sand from under my feet, it *grabbed me, too—dragging me out to sea! Total terror—I screamed. Strong arms snatched me back, hauled me up into a warm broad chest, and held me close until I stopped whimpering and could relax. That's what daddies do.*

I sigh as I walk, wanting more. I have only these snapshots: the beach, going fishing once when I was five and crying when I realized "the fishies" died, and the times he came home from work with little packages of gummy worms for me and my friends. Nothing else is clear. I wish I could remember him in everyday memories, like Michael does.

I know he worked for Hewlett-Packard and didn't much like his job, because that's what my mom has told me. I vaguely remember when he got laid off and how weird it was having him home. I know sometimes he drank, and I remember how my brother got up and walked out of the room when Mom told us he was sick. I was thirteen, and it was summer. She said, "Cancer," her face broke into pieces, and my brain swirled out of control—I couldn't slow it down enough to catch details.

We changed the living room into his bedroom because it was bigger and the hospital bed would fit. Hospice nurses came and went. Michael spent lots of time with his best friend, Steve. My eighth-grade year started. I got my very first-ever period and told my best friend, Ginny. I remember not telling my mom because it didn't seem very important.

He died a few weeks later, at night. I was sleeping. Michael was at Steve's.

Mom called the funeral home and waited by herself until they came, then took one of his sleeping pills and crawled into bed in their old room. When I got up for school and tiptoed down the hall like I always did, her door was shut and the air was perfectly still. Before I realized the living room was empty, before I even turned on the light to see for sure, I knew.

The bed had been stripped and pushed to the side. His robe was folded on top. The table where his meds had sat was empty—the prescription bottles and other paraphernalia swept off into a plastic bag tied with a knot and dropped on the floor. I felt like something had sucked my insides out; I remember wondering how I could be so completely empty and still able to stand up. I stood paralyzed—my brain registering details as my thoughts rolled themselves out in slow motion:

My father is dead.

I will never see my father again.

This couldn't have happened.

It's happened.

I won't ever hear his voice.

I'll never touch him.

My father is dead. . . .

I will never see my father. . . .

. . . and endlessly on.

I knew right then there was no way in the entire world I could live through this. No way at all.

Except, I did.

One hour after the next, and then a day and a week, a month, a year, and now—just about exactly two.

FIVE

I'm cast.

I'm Maggie.

I'm in the play.

The list is posted in the hallway of the theater. I cannot believe I am actually seeing my name—I check it five times. Nine parts, nine actors, one A.D.—and *one of them is me*. First rehearsal is this afternoon.

All day long, I'm new. Nothing can bother me. I don't care if people talk to me or if I have a place to sit at snack. I kinda like that I get a dirty look from two older girls walking by, because I remember them from the audition. At snack Layla says, "Congratulations." My hippie-biker science teacher pats me on the shoulder and tells me he heard I got into the play. I go to the theater at lunch to pick up my script. Tess gives me a huge hug. I manage the entire day without running into anything. At three fifteen, I'm sitting in a circle with six other kids I don't know, and the Hollywood Three.

"Keep it simple and keep it true," Tess warns. She twists her long hair into a knot in the back of her head and sticks a pencil through. "This play cannot be melodramatic. Find the humor."

"Right, that should be easy," says David, the guy playing my husband.

I don't know the play, but I laugh with everyone else. We read. I am taken into the story so completely it's hard to believe almost two hours go by before we close our scripts.

"Damn, Tess," Jake says. "We're doing a play on death."

"I don't think so," David argues.

"Everybody's dying, dawg, what do *you* think it's about?" Jake challenges him.

"Life, basically."

I don't say anything, but I agree with David.

Rehearsal's over, and I have time to be amazed at how good all the actors are. I can't help but smile at them as we pack up. Everybody but Stacey smiles back. She obviously doesn't like that I got into the play, and right now I don't particularly care. The girl playing Layla's mother introduces herself—her name is Frazier. David tells me I'm an amazing actor and offers me a ride home. He figures we should get to know each other since we're going to be husband and wife. The assistant director hands us each a rehearsal schedule, and Tess gives me a hug as we leave.

In the car David explains he's been at this school for three years and that he had mono in tenth grade, which is why he's in eleventh grade now instead of twelfth. I tell him my life story, at least the part about my mom getting remarried to a Beverly Hills accountant and us moving into a huge house in Brentwood. He asks if I miss all my friends from Santa Rosa. I lie and tell him yes, and then I make him laugh by describing my asshole brother. I figure talking about my dad can wait until I know him better. He offers me a ride to school in the morning, since he only lives four blocks away. I say sure and we pull up in front of my house.

I have to blink a couple times before I go into the house and realize this is, indeed, major. I have gotten a lead in the play. A boy has driven me home. My smile is *so* connected, I think I must have discovered my real self.

SIX

Michael's pissed. My way-cool, nothing-ever-bothers-me jock of a brother is stomping around like a two-year-old throwing a tantrum. I hear him slam the front door and pound up the stairs to his room, across from mine. He slams that door too, then turns on the awful hard rock noise he calls music. I go back to my laptop, adding screen names to my "buddy list" from the e-mail addresses the A.D. typed up so the cast can get in touch with each other.

Mom and Robert come in about twenty minutes later, and Mrs. Hoyt, the housekeeper (we have a housekeeper!) calls us for dinner. It's the first time in a week we've eaten together. Mom is beaming, and she and Robert are acting like they always do— giddy. He's got to be twenty years older than her and I can't imagine him running anything, let alone his own million-dollar accounting firm. Of course, I only see him around my mom, and I seriously doubt he's ever had a girlfriend as pretty as her. She's certainly never had a guy as rich as him, at least that she's told *us* about. It's disgusting when your mother acts like she's in eighth grade.

Michael comes late to the table, and for some reason I get a flash of our dad, even though I don't think Michael particularly looks like him. Whatever's going on, being around Robert doesn't help. Michael's face is closed and stormy. He's scary when he's like this because you can't tell what he's thinking and he won't admit to anything. I decide to hold on to my casting news until later.

Mrs. Hoyt brings food. Mom and Robert chatter about going to Cabo for their honeymoon. Michael eats quietly and quickly, mumbles "Excuse me," and pushes back from the table.

"Why don't you wait until we're all finished, son?" Robert asks.

Michael mumbles rather than speaks, staring down at the floor. "Well, for one thing, I'm not your son."

It's silent at the table. Mom sighs and picks at her plate. Robert does the please-remember-this-is-my-house transformation and glares meaningfully at my brother.

"Sorry," Michael grunts. "I had a bad day, okay?"

"Happens to all of us," Robert says. He's entirely too reasonable to be part of this family. "Sit down. We'll talk about it."

"Nothing to talk about." Michael smiles his tight, awful smile, the one he got after our father died. He wants to snap back at my mom like he used to; instead, he sits down. Rules have changed since we moved to Robert's.

"How were tryouts?" Mom asks him. She's hopeful it will be this easy.

"Didn't go."

Robert is surprisingly wise and doesn't respond. Mom is startled. "But I thought you—"

"No summer practice, no varsity team. That's the rule."

"But we didn't live here this summer," I blurt.

"Yeah. Well. I don't really care. The team sucks." Michael's face is out of balance somehow. "Am I done?"

Robert nods almost imperceptibly, except we all see, and Mom nods out loud. Michael leaves. I think I'll save my news for tomorrow or maybe next year, because I've just now realized that last night was the second anniversary of when our father died—if anniversary is what you call it.

How could I not know that?

The pain is unexpected; it almost knocks me over.

My father is dead—I will never see my father again—this could not have happened. . . .

I look at my mom talking with Robert. I see the last of Michael going up the stairs.

Did they cry?

Once, each of them, that I remember.

Did we talk about my dad?

No.

We did the wake and the funeral and then . . . then nothing is very clear. I shake my head slightly and sigh. Mom jerks her attention over to me with a not-you-too look on her face.

Playing Clueless But Happy Girl, I smile and ask for the potatoes.

SEVEN

Saturday rehearsals and here I am—gossiping with the popular girls as the boys are inside running lines. Oh wait. No I'm not. They're gossiping. I'm pretending they know I'm here.

At least I'm smiling.

"Why is this so hard for you?" Frazier teases, throwing her hands up. "'Friends with benefits'? Give me a break."

"It can work," Layla counters. "Look at whatshername—Kelly, and that guy John."

"PDA addiction. People who sleep around are sluts."

Layla laughs. "So that's every guy we know?"

Frazier pops a Famous Amos into her mouth. "And some girls," she says. Layla sits up straighter.

"Please," Frazier mumbles, mouth full of cookie. "She's out of control and you know it. At Sophia's. That guy from UCLA. Whatshisname from Crossroads. Should I go on?"

Layla glances in my direction, but I've managed to drop my head over my script. She turns her attention back to Frazier. "Maybe you should just shut up."

"Yeah, well maybe you should be her friend and say something."

The line is a cue. A black Jag swerves into the parking space next to us and Stacey slides out. She slams the door, doesn't say good-bye to her dad or whoever it is driving, and stomps straight into the theater. Frazier grabs another cookie. Layla follows Stacey inside.

I have a hugely bad feeling, like glass in the pit of my stomach. Like seeing my mother's face for the first time after my dad died. Like Michael's energy at the dinner table. Something's happened with Stacey and, whatever it is, I think I understand. Except how it is that possible? I don't even know the girl.

Frazier keeps enjoying her cookies. Layla yells for us to come back in. I expect we'll find out now that some tragedy's occurred: Stacey's mother has died or, at the very least, a grandmother or something. I'll step up and smile in the way you can when you know how someone feels. Maybe even help.

We're running act one, first time off book. We don't have to stay onstage when the other scenes are working, so I watch Stacey carefully, to pick up on the subtext. Since I know about death firsthand, this might be worth something. Except Stacey seems *fine*, even more brilliant than usual onstage. And offstage she chats with Layla and teases Jake and ignores me, and I am thankful at least for that, and for the fact that I managed not to actually open my mouth.

Because Stupid Kate has appeared full force, reminding me that I could never ever have anything in common with a *Vogue* model.

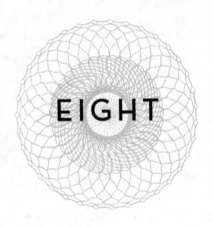

EIGHT

Jake is having a cast party. And we haven't even opened.

I'm invited.

As much as I try to pretend it's no big deal ("Sure, I can go, whatever"), nothing this huge has ever happened in my heretofore Nonexistent Social Life. I talk myself out of it and back into it forty times before Friday:

I'll have fun.

I'll feel stupid.

I won't know what to say.

I have nothing to wear.

SO WHAT, I GOT INVITED and I'M GOING.

I'll have fun. . . .

Endless little circles of insecurity. At long last the Universe takes pity on me and makes Frazier invite me over so we can get ready together. She wants to help me do my makeup and straighten my hair. I don't usually wear makeup but Frazier thinks I should, and who am I to interfere with divine judgment?

Michael tries to get me to say exactly where it is. He wants to crash it so he "can meet that hot redhead you hang out with." How little he knows! I'm not worried because even if he came, he'd know how to act, but I'm guessing he won't really even try. He's not as sure of himself in LA as he was in Santa Rosa.

Mom almost messes things up by changing her mind at the last minute. Robert (of all people!) intervenes. "I know the boy's family," he assures her. "They're fine people."

I've almost gotten used to the opulence of Brentwood, but it's a ghetto compared to Lexington Road in Beverly Hills, which is wider than Santa Rosa's Highway 12. This is not a street—it's a *boulevard.* There are no *houses*, there are *estates.* Jake's is behind a ten-foot-tall hedge that takes up the entire side of one block.

My first clue that we may not be going to your average small cast party comes when Frazier has to park two blocks away. Second subtle hint—two security guards in front of the gate, which you would never find if you didn't know where to look. Third—we pass two dozen people in the yard who I've never seen before, and I've seen pretty much everyone at Bentley Evans Prep. The Universe has tricked me again.

Music is blasting. We walk by a couple attached at the hip on the bench by the fountain and Frazier points and mouths, "Slut." Two extremely skinny girls wearing more makeup than clothes strut up the stairs. On the deck Stacey's dancing with a tall dark-haired *man* who's got to be, minimum, twenty-five. Layla's standing with a bunch of guys I've seen around school but don't know. She and Frazier do the hug thing. Frazier and the boys do the hug thing. No one does the hug thing with me so I just stand there, *smiling.*

Of course.

Stacey pushes the guy away from her. "I said no." She leaves him there with his dick in his hand (not really, it was a champagne bottle), and Layla laughs at him as she loops her arms through Frazier's.

"Come, children, let's get you a beverage." She looks back at me. "Oh, Maggie, good, you came. Jesus Christ, you're not Maggie, are you, you're . . . oh shit . . ." She slurs her words. "You're Katie! Katie-katie! Come on, Katie. Come with us."

Still smiling, I trail them through the party, into the kitchen, where Layla pours us each a glass of champagne.

"*Sip* it," she advises me, waggling her finger in my direction. "You are too young to drink, so go slow." She giggles and disappears with Frazier into the crowd. The last I see of them is Frazier motioning me to come along, but I shake my head and smile harder. I sip my drink, but I actually have never had alcohol before and it tastes really bad. David comes over but doesn't stay when we figure out we've got nothing to say to each other that isn't about the play.

I wander. I pretend to drink. I smile at people and say "Hey," but the most I get back is a brief nod-almost-smile from a girl in my acting class. My brain dissolves to mush and my new Briefly Confident Self slides into the murk. Stupid Kate takes stage, right on cue, and finds me a place on a couch in one of the living rooms so I can wait it out. At least I have makeup and straight hair—I can *look* like I'm part of things.

"Where the hell is Jake?" Frazier demands of the room. Her face is pale, and she's louder than the party. I try to figure out how long I've been sitting here.

"Hey yo," Jake calls from over by the corner, and they head for the stairs.

"Stacey passed out and we can't hear her breathing. . . ." Frazier's trying to whisper now, but the room's gone silent and we all hear and surge up the stairs after her. Stacey's guy from the porch is pacing in the upstairs hallway.

"Shit, Jake—I didn't know, man . . ." he manages to gasp. Stacey's on the bed with her shirt open and her jeans unzipped. She isn't wearing a bra. And she sure isn't moving.

"Is she dead, bro?" the guy whines. "Shit. Is she dead?"

Layla shoves past and then turns and starts pushing people out of the room. "What's the matter with you? Get out of here!" She turns on the porch guy, hitting him in the chest as she talks. "What did you give her? *What did you give her?*" Jake is dialing 9-1-1.

"OxyContin."

"*What?!*" Layla's a tornado. "Are you stupid?"

"Hey, she said she wanted it. But then she just passed out, man, and I couldn't wake her up," the guy says.

"You knew she was drinking, you asshole!" Layla's trying to get Stacey up. Jake is still talking into the phone, saying "OxyContin" and "champagne" and then listening.

"She's got to throw up," he announces. "Get her in the bathroom." More people pour in to see what's happening. Jake keeps snapping out orders. "Wake her up, keep her moving. Don't let her go to sleep. She needs to throw up. . . ."

"Shit, will somebody please help me?" Layla yells. Frazier steps forward and they somehow manage to get Stacey up and into the bathroom. Frazier turns on the tap and splashes cold water on Stacey's cheeks. Stacey groans. Layla slaps her, not gently, and Stacey moves her head and groans again. Her eyelids flutter. Layla slaps her one more time. I stand in the bathroom door, trying to block everyone out. Stacey's conscious now, but limp.

"Stick your finger down your throat," Layla orders, but Stacey doesn't seem to understand. Her eyelids flutter and she slumps forward. "Shit! Jake! Help me!"

Jake and Frazier hold Stacey up and Layla pushes her own finger down the back of Stacey's throat. Nothing happens, except *I* gag. She does it again. Stacey's eyes fly wide open and vomit shoots up and out and all over her and Layla. Jake and Frazier lower her down to her knees, and she heaves into the toilet. Now I seriously want to throw up. But suddenly there are sirens outside and people in a hurry. Stacey sits back on her knees, exhausted and weak, leaning on the edge of the toilet. She starts to cry, making little kitten sounds; Layla kneels down to hug her, whispering, "It's okay, honey, it's okay. . . ."

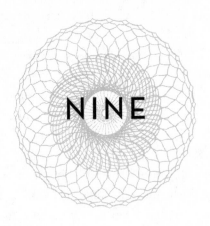

NINE

This house is so big, I might as well be home alone. I want to go talk to somebody, but my mom is on another planet whenever she's with her husband-to-be, and Michael is out somewhere with who knows who, doing whatever sad, pissed-off seventeen-year-old boys do. Besides, what the hell would I say?

Gee, Mom, it's like I'm watching a movie but I'm in it too. Everything's slow motion, except my heartbeat, which has doubled—and it feels just like ninth grade!

This would guarantee the why-don't-you-ever-talk-to-me-am-I-a-bad-mother? conversation, which would not help in the least. So I mull it alone: two fire trucks, an ambulance—the entire block lit with flashing red lights. Kids streaming out, screeching off a Vin Diesel movie, security guards nowhere to be seen. Then cops, and Frazier grabbing my hand and Layla's: we bolt, hiding in a hedge down the street to watch Stacey being carried out on a gurney and her and Jake speeding away in an ambulance.

"Close one," Frazier mumbles.

"You have no idea," Layla mumbles back. I'm not really there, so I don't say a word.

In the car I expect we'll talk about it. I have fifty thousand questions—one of which is why the hell does an incredibly beautiful and talented girl like Stacey get so out of control? But the conversation veers immediately to the mundane, and it takes me all the way to my house to figure out maybe they just don't want to talk about it with *me*.

Leaving me with entirely too much information and none at all. Is this to be the theme of my life? I get food from the kitchen and try to watch TV in the den, except the room is spooking me and I can't concentrate. I pace awhile and end up in my bedroom. Where I sit and worry—about Stacey, but mostly about myself. Because why do I care about this girl who hates me? I pace more. I go online to look for information, and find out Stacey could easily have died.

Stuff like this did not happen in Santa Rosa. Or, if it did, nobody told me. I get chills thinking about it; Stacey could have been a story on the eleven o'clock news. Just then, the computer dings and the instant message box pops up.

bratgurl444 has sent you an instant message.
Do you wish to accept?

It's Julia, the A.D. from the show. I hit Okay.

bratgurl444: were u there?
kt13: where?
bratgurl444: at jake's.
kt13: yeah. were u?
bratgurl444: no. did u see what happened?

30

Another box pops up: "SweetLayla."

> sweetlayla: hi katie. it's frazier. u ok?
> kt13: i'm fine. u?
> sweetlayla: we're gd. tired.

Julia dings:

> bratgurl444: r u there?
> kt13: yeah. sry.
> bratgurl444: what happened to stacey?

Frazier at Layla's:

> sweetlayla: do me a favor, ok? don't talk to anybody about
> stace
> kt13: k
> sweetlayla: ur cool. thanks.

Julia:

> bratgurl444: katie? who else r u talking 2?

To Frazier/Layla:

> kt13: no problem. is stacey ok?

Julia:

> bratgurl444: u there
> bratgurl444: i heard she tried to commit suicide
> kt13: who did?

To Frazier/Layla:

> kt13: is stacey okay?
> kt13: frazier?
> kt13: julia says stacey tried to commit suicide!

Julia:

> bratgurl444: stacey. who else?
> bratgurl444: i thought u said u were there.

A box appears:

> User sweetlayla is no longer signed on.

Julia:

> kt13: i was but I don't think that happened.
> bratgurl444: didn't u see the ambulance?
> kt13: no.
> bratgurl444: r u telling me the truth?
> kt13: no, i'm lying. what do u think?
> bratgurl444: whatever. g2g.
> kt13: k. bye.
> bratgurl444: they won't be ur friends, even if u protect her.

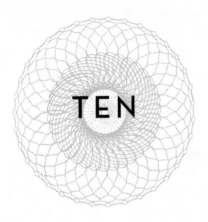

TEN

Tess doesn't know if we can do the play. This isn't the first time Stacey's had trouble with substance abuse, and the school may kick her out. For now she's suspended, and her dad has called a lawyer. We can't recast—we're too far along. We can't reschedule—the flyers have all gone out. The deans are phoning the parents of everyone they think was there to let them know what happened. No one's mentioned suicide.

"It wasn't a *school* party," Jake argues. He's pissed and doesn't care who knows it. "They have absolutely no right to punish her."

"The *police* notified the school, Jake," Tess tells us. "Stacey's parents were out of town. The housekeeper gave them our number."

"They still don't have the right—" Jake's on a rant.

"It doesn't matter, does it?" Tess interrupts. "It's done."

Layla shakes her head. "This is so not fair. We called 9-1-1—"

"What's 'so not fair' is that Stacey got high. She put herself, all of you, and our show in jeopardy," Tess says. I nod my head before I realize I'm doing it. Jake starts to protest, but Tess holds up her hand and glares at him. I've never seen her like this. "And your parents should have been home."

"Tess—" Layla starts to say.

Tess shakes her head. "No. No more discussion." She stands and doesn't even try to smile. "Rehearsals are canceled until we find out what's going to happen. Now go away, please. Check the board tomorrow."

Time loops back to before I got cast in the play and drops me smack in the middle of the Isolation Ward. I spend the entire morning without talking, until the dean of students sidles up at snack and wants to know my version of what happened. He says he's talking to everyone. I say I saw the ambulance and the cops and left. I say I never ran into Stacey again after I first saw her on the porch. He nods but doesn't believe a word.

All day the party's the main topic of conversation and we "theater kids" are heavily scrutinized. The rumors are vicious— obviously I'm not the only one who's felt Stacey's wrath. Frazier and Layla and Jake escape off campus, but I'm stuck; tenth graders can't leave till they're done with classes. I hide out in the greenroom. Tess shuts her office door and I'm alone until David joins me.

"Hey."

"Do you think she tried to kill herself?" He half whispers it.

I shrug. "You'd know better than me. You've been here longer."

"Hey, I don't hang out with them." He laughs a little.

It suddenly strikes me that David could have left campus too, but instead he's here, with me. I'm suddenly shy.

"I just thought, well, never mind. . . ." I fumble. "And Stacey is so beautiful. . . ."

"Whoa, hold on. *Beautiful?*"

"You don't think so?"

"Maybe if you're into concentration camps."

We talk through lunch. He drives me home after school and I almost ask if he wants to come in. It's weird to be home by three thirty. Weirder to know that David doesn't think Stacey is hot. He likes to talk to me. Right. Like *that* would ever happen. Still, I can't get him off my mind.

Until I am summoned for the Talk.

"I knew this wouldn't work." My mother paces as she rants. She's obviously gotten the Phone Call. Robert listens patiently and Michael hovers. He's been up and down the stairs at least three times. I expect he's there to laugh at me.

"The social thing here is way too fast. Way—too—fast. These kids have too much money and no supervision, and they're too old for Kaitlyn to hang out with."

"They're just a year or two older, Mom," Michael pipes up, to everyone's surprise.

"I don't recall inviting you to this conversation," Mom retorts.

"Since when do I need an invitation?"

"Michael—"

"Katie's in tenth grade. She can handle this."

Is the Universe taunting me? Is this my own asshole brother, being a nice guy? Mom continues as if he never spoke.

"I am not going to have a repeat of last year. If this isn't working, I want to know now. I don't want things sneaking up on me again."

"It's no different anywhere else," Robert says quietly. I suddenly remember he has two grown daughters and wonder why we've never met them. "Kate simply went to the party. She wasn't the one whisked off to the hospital."

"She still should have told us about it."

All eyes turn in my direction. I shrug. And did I mention? Smile.

"You should have told us," Mom repeats. "How am I supposed to trust you now?"

"Oh please," Michael says in a remarkably easy tone. "You're not exactly accessible these days."

"I don't know if this is really your business, Mike," Robert says in an equally easy voice, "or mine, either, actually. Let's let your mother handle it."

"My sister, my business," Michael says with a shrug. His voice still sounds pleasant and there's no tight little smile. Maybe because it's not about him?

"All right. Fair enough," Robert says. "What do you think we should do?"

"Get over it. Shit happens."

"It does not happen in this family," my mother insists.

"Mom, Katie didn't OD. She didn't take any drugs and I bet she didn't even drink. She got somebody to bring her home. What else was she supposed to do?"

I am now truly shocked. Michael is 100 percent on my side.

"She should have told us about it," my mother repeats.

"Please. Get real." Michael makes a face at her. "How much did you tell *your* parents?"

My mother sighs and her body relaxes a little. "Okay, maybe you're right, but Katie . . . you have no idea how worried I was last year. And this is—"

I find words! "*So* different, Mom. I swear."

"Is it? Really? Because we haven't had a chance to talk much since we've been down here. . . ."

I think: Uh, Mom, we have never "talked."

I say: "It's fine, I'm good. I like the school. . . . I'm making friends. And the play is awesome."

"If there is a play," she reminds me.

"Right. Well, I'm hoping there will be."

"Okay. But do you promise this time you'll let me know if something's going wrong?"

I avoid looking at Michael's twinkly eyes and nod my head. "I promise."

ELEVEN

The Official Word: Stacey will come back to rehearsal at the beginning of next week.

The Rumors: The school wanted to kick her out, but her lawyers threatened to sue; she will be only allowed back after she completes a drug and alcohol rehab program; her parents are hiring a full-time therapist to move into their house; her grandfather is donating $500,000 to the school. No doubt Jake and Layla know the real story, but they're not talking.

Tess asks me to take the "Beverly" blocking for her. I don't particularly want to, but I'm the only one completely off book and besides—I am a True Actor. I'll do anything for the play. Every day that week I run my scenes with David and I do Stacey's scenes with Jake and Gabe. I notice people seem to have a lot more fun with each other when Stacey's not here. I also notice how very much I like the fact that David waits around and drives me home.

On Friday Stacey comes to watch. I am so completely into the Mark and Beverly scene that I don't notice her slipping in.

We finish the scene; I look to Tess for notes, and there sits the Drama Queen, in all her skinny regal redness. Layla calls out, "Stace!" and everyone swarms around her, even Tess of the no-more-discussion-I-am-really-pissed attitude. Only David stands his ground and, of course, me.

Roles are reversed. Where Stacey did not feel it necessary to applaud when I worked, I do not deem it necessary to fawn over her. I sit on the set and start copying today's work into the script I'm keeping for her. I look up and, witchlike, she's appeared.

"So is that mine?" she asks, holding out her hand. These may be the first words she's spoken directly to me.

"Yeah." I even manage not to smile. "I marked the—"

"Great. Thanks." She snatches it and heads for the door. Jake and Layla join her on the way out.

"You're welcome," I mutter loud enough for only me to hear. "Anytime. Glad to do it. Fifteen hours' extra work? Hey—for *you*, not a problem."

A blink and it's tech week. We spend Saturday writing cues, standing in places, and waiting for the lights to be set. It's boring and long and tedious and, basically, the essence of my life. I love every single second. It doesn't matter anymore who likes who—or doesn't; we're a company and we have a play to do. Even Stacey's acting okay—I haven't had a dirty look from her in days.

Suddenly it's opening night. An hour before curtain Tess takes us down to the dance studio for warm-up and focus. She plays music and turns the lights low and has us walk without relating to anyone, just concentrating on who we are in the play. I know without a second of doubt that this is what it feels like to be *happy*.

"Invite your character in," Tess directs, and I feel Katie slipping off to the side and Maggie taking her place. The overwhelming fear of knowing my husband is dying starts to dictate the way my body moves, how I look at David and little Matt, the sixth grader who is playing my son, even how I sip my coffee. I imagine pain in the area around my heart, and the rest of me closes in as protection. I'm vaguely aware of the same phenomenon occurring to the actors around me. Tess moves us through the work and leads us back to the theater. Before I can grapple with the sounds of the audience settling in, places are called and we begin.

The Shadow Box is even more powerful onstage than I expected. "Beverly" and "Brian" and "Mark" rage and fight, and the tears that spring to "Mark's" eyes after "Beverly" slaps him are not from the pain of the slap. I, "Maggie," resist and finally break under the relentless pressure to accept the fact that "Joe" is dying. "Agnes" realizes that all her efforts to help "Felicity" only prolong her suffering. Finally we face the audience together—changed—and play the final scene.

Music starts, lights fade to blackout, a second of absolute silence—then, applause. Lights come up and the audience actually stands. People are wiping their eyes. We hit the greenroom and David lets out a bloodcurdling cheer, startling us into laughter, forcing us back to ourselves. Frazier hugs me. David hugs me. Everyone starts changing, right in front of each other, as they babble about the play. Even little Matt has something to say. Bereft of Maggie, I stand mute. No one notices. I pick up my street clothes and duck into the bathroom.

Outside, kids from the school and people I don't even know stop to tell me how good I was. I'm still trying to figure out how to be myself, connect, and enjoy this part of the process. Michael grabs me and hugs me.

"Who knew?" he whispers, and shoves a dozen roses at me.

My brother is actually embarrassed! I want the right thing to say back to him, but I'm too slow. He gives me a quick kiss on the cheek and makes his escape.

Mom and Robert stand off to the side, grinning like they could bust open. I keep finding eyes of other cast members and, despite my determination not to care if they acknowledge me, I love how everyone smiles back. Tess tells me how happy she is that I came to Bentley Evans. David wraps his arms around me from behind. My mom grins even more and heads toward me.

"We're all going to my house," David whispers in my ear.

"I don't think I can," I say back.

"Can what, honey?" Mom asks, joining us.

"I'm having the cast over," David announces, backing off from his bear hug. His voice changes a little. I don't think I've ever heard him this polite. "I was seeing if Kate wanted to come."

Frazier slips her arm through mine. "Yeah, come on, Katie, it won't be very late. We have a show tomorrow."

"Where do you live?" Robert asks.

"Are your parents home?" my mom says at the same time.

I see Stacey behind them, rolling her eyes. "Actually, they're not," David says, in that same courteous manner, "but my house-keeper is. And I just live over on Avondale."

"That's close," says Robert.

"It's just the cast. We're ordering pizza," Frazier says. "Tell me when you want Kate home and I'll make sure she's there." She's acquired the same charming personality.

"You're welcome to come too, if you want," David adds. I happen to catch the expression that flits over Frazier's face and realize David is scamming my mom. And it's working.

She smiles at him and talks to me. "Okay, but home by one, all right?"

"Absolutely," David answers. "I'll make sure of it."

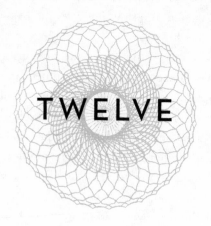

TWELVE

In my new Normal and Connected Life, I'm squished in the backseat of a black BMW with the popular kids of an exclusive private school, after the successful opening of an incredible play in which I played a lead.

Oh wait—it's really true.

We're rehashing the moments—the mistakes as well as the triumphs—and laughing about them all. At least they're rehashing. I'm mostly smiling, but since I'm actually tremendously happy right now, the smile fits. What a breakthrough. Maybe soon I'll have something to say.

David's house is low, long, and large. It wraps almost completely around a pool and pool house with a laid-back kind of feeling. We end up in his rec room, and I realize I'm actually getting used to houses like this—big-screen, flat TV mounted on the wall, pool table, three couches, and a bar. A completely alien world from Santa Rosa, and I'm liking it. David sets out two six-packs of beer and holds up a videotape.

"Oh shit, how'd you do that?" Layla says.

"Yeah, well, what Tess doesn't know, huh?"

"I love this boy," Frazier announces.

I think I do too. People settle in on the couches or the floor in front. I have one of those horrible moments of not knowing where to sit, but David pats the space next to him. "Come, 'wife.'" On the way over I do not once even *almost* trip or come *near* to crashing into something. In celebration of that victory, I grab a beer. Normal, right?

"I hate this," Layla complains. "I cannot stand myself on film."

"I don't blame you," Jake teases. She smacks him.

The focus is off in places and you can't see faces clearly, but all in all, the tape isn't too bad. We fast-forward through lots of it, but it's fun, and at least I don't look stupid. I hold the beer in my hand and pretend to sip it a couple of times. David drops his arm around me and I sit there smiling. I try to think if I've said even one word and start to drink the beer for real. It almost makes me gag, it tastes so vile. I make myself chug it, almost half of the whole thing at one time. Stacey's watching. I burp, loudly, and giggle. She toasts me from her side of the couch.

"Omigod," she says, "maybe you *are* human."

I smile at her, toast her back, then drink the rest of it down. The room sways slightly and I giggle again—this time at how light-headed I feel. David smiles and hands me another.

I can't concentrate on the TV anymore. My eyes want to close and my head keeps nodding forward. I end up snuggling down inside David's arm, with my head on his chest. I can hear people talking. I feel close to every damn person in this room. We did an amazing show and now we're enjoying ourselves. It's easy to get along with people when you relax.

"Kate?"

I open my eyes and the room swerves like a car around a curve, so I giggle and close them again. "Mm-hmm?" I say.

"Oh man, she's wasted," Layla says.

"She only had one beer," Frazier says.

"Why do I think it's her first one ever?" Jake asks.

"Leave her alone, you guys," David's voice answers. "She'll be fine."

"Yeah, but her mom said be home by one," Layla says. "It's quarter to."

"I don't wanna go home," I whine, enjoying the fact that words are tumbling out of me, even if they do sound a tiny bit slurred. I love this attention. I love the ease with which I'm getting it. "I wanna pee."

"I'll take her," Frazier says, and the next thing I know I'm upright and walking. Then I'm alone in a bathroom, looking at myself in the mirror.

"Whoa." I say it out loud but it's like someone else is talking. There we are, me and Stupid Kate—and one of us is stuck in the mirror. I giggle as I wonder which one, then I start to disappear. Suddenly dizzy, I slide down to sit on the toilet and hang my head down between my knees. I've slipped over some edge and it isn't fun now. Somehow I manage to finish peeing and get my hands washed and open the door. David's waiting to walk me back.

We settle back on the couch, I lean my head on his chest and drift. Someone calls my mom and tells her the pizza took too long to get there and we're just now starting to eat. I glance up and see everything is normal. The TV is playing some kind of old science fiction. Layla and Stacey and Jake are piled on each other, laughing at it. Frazier and Gabe have gone. The panic drains out and I drift some more.

I dream that David is kissing me.

I wonder what time it is.

I realize David *is* kissing me. And I like it.

"Coffee," Layla's voice says. David sits me up a little and puts a cup in my hand. "Just sip a little," she tells me. "It's not too hot."

I swallow a gulp and make a face.

"You are so cute," Layla says. "You remind me of me in seventh grade, I swear to God. Doesn't she?" I smile and take another sip of the coffee. I like being cute. I don't know yet about private school double-talk and I think she means it. I almost like being drunk.

"Careful, babe," David warns, and puts his hand on the side of my head to draw me back to his chest.

"What a good little girl you are, Kate," Stacey says, that echo of sarcasm in her voice.

"Fuck off, okay?" David says, and strokes my hair back from my face. He leans in to kiss me again. Unfortunately, the coffee isn't compatible with the beer and I'm going to hurl. I scramble up, dash to the bathroom, and vomit my entire gut into the toilet. Do I remember to shut the door? Of course not. Vaguely I'm aware of people piling in behind me, but too bad, I hurl again. Somebody grabs my hair back and flushes the toilet every once in a while, cooing in a low voice, "It's okay, it's okay, Katie, just get it out. Get it out."

Which I do. Which clears my brain. Which lets me realize how extraordinarily stupid I look. But wait—can I smile now, because this would be a good time to smile? No. I cry. In front of all the people in the world that I want to impress, I sit on the goddamn floor of a bathroom and cry.

"Hey, Katie-katie, it's no big deal," Layla says, running a wet washcloth over my face. "Stace does it all the time." Even Stacey laughs at that one.

The hallway stretches forever and this time the walls are closing in and the Monster's already used up all the air. Minnie Mouse swoops down to save me and suddenly we're floating and I can breathe. I see Michael below waving but the Monster gobbles him up and Minnie disappears. I start to fall. The Monster snatches me before I hit the ground and bites me into two people. One is inside him; the other is outside, screaming. Minnie swoops in again, but this time she wraps duct tape around my face, leaving only my eyes connected to the outside.

THIRTEEN

So, the show's over and it's like it never happened; I'm Invisible New Girl again. Amazing True Actor has melted into the cast picture posted on the theater "memory wall," and I have nothing to say to people I've worked with every day for the past two months. I pretend I don't see Stacey and her bitch-stare. I smile when I run into random objects that everyone else in the entire world is able to miss. I skulk past David, *the guy who was kissing me*, instead of asking when he's going to call me—*like he said he would backstage on closing night.* Oh, by the way, which is when he kissed me again.

Ah, Stupid Kate. How I've missed her.

Jake has another party, for Stacey's eighteenth. I am not invited; no doubt Stacey reminded him that all I do at parties is sit around or throw up. Or—substantially worse—he simply didn't remember to think of me. I don't even know about it until after it happens, when everyone who *went* needs to say to everyone who didn't: *"Omigod, you weren't invited??"*

I smile and shrug. *Omigod, can't you go die somewhere??*

To make the world perfect, Thanksgiving break arrives and Michael flies up to Steve's for the entire *five*-day weekend. I'm stuck at home with an overage glamour queen I used to call "Mom" and a middle-aged man who prances through the house like a horny twelve-year-old. Add the geometry homework from hell, a six-page research paper on a line from a poem by some dead gay guy I've never heard of, and—this is the biggest bummer of all—no show to look forward to.

"Completely sucks" is the descriptive phrase I've chosen.

Somehow I survive Thanksgiving dinner, managing to find random acts of kindness to be thankful for, which I express in the briefest of terms so Mom and Robert can get back to being thankful for each other. After dessert I plead homework and hide in my room to go online. I find a site on schizophrenia and it's actually making a lot of sense on a very personal level, especially the part about "onset with adolescence," when Layla IMs me to go to a movie with her and then sleep over at her house.

Whoa.

There is no logical reason for her to want to spend time with me. I say I have to check with my mom. She says, "k, cool, let me know." I sign off and freak out more. What's going on? Does she feel bad Jake didn't invite me to his party? Not likely. Is it some kind of setup? I've seen it done now at school a couple of times, but Layla doesn't seem the type. Maybe everyone else is out of town. I've heard her say how she hates to be in her house alone.

The Universe chuckles at my dilemma: if I go, Stupid Kate will show up and Layla will wish she'd called someone else. I'll become fodder for half-whispered conversations, a guaranteed social disaster. If I don't, I'll be stuck here alone with middle-aged hormones and my own very split personality.

No contest.

I lie and say I'm going out of town. Then I sign off. I'm not in the mood for any more of the outside world, and the big screen downstairs has nine billion channels. Plus there's all that homework to do. And earphones were made for blocking what you don't want to hear.

Here's the list: the two weeks after Thanksgiving are ridiculously busy and I'm probably the only person in the school's history who manages to go from a low B to "watch out, Brainless," in both geometry and World Civ.

Which makes Robert hire a tutor.

Which effectively eliminates free time after school or in the upcoming winter break.

However! Nightmares are down, I now dress in a relatively cool-yet-individual manner, my hair is looking great—and, oh, about the no free time? It doesn't matter! I have no show, no friends, and no life—I have nothing to do *but* study.

"Wanna ride home?" David says, and I look over my shoulder to see who he's talking to. This is the same David who has not remembered I'm alive the past week or so. He smiles, and suddenly I don't care. "You, Katie. Do you want a ride home?"

"Oh, sorry, I thought . . ." I blush, giggle. . . . "Sure. Yeah. Thanks."

He tosses my backpack into his car and we slide in. "Hey, where have you been lately?"

"Um . . . oh, just around." *Good, Kate—*

"School sure sucks, doesn't it?"

"Yeah, um . . ." *Speak!*

"So what are you doing over break?"

"Me? Um, not much." *Why am I so lame?*

"Well, I was kinda wondering if maybe you wanna go to Aspen with me?"

"Um . . . what?" I almost look over my shoulder again, as my heart does this strange little turning over in the chest affair. *I wonder if he's making fun of me.*

"My whole family goes. We have a house and basically just ski and hang out. You have to share a room with my sister but she's cool. What do you think?"

"Uh . . ." *Maybe he means it?*

"Hey, if you don't want to, it's okay. I understand."

"No, no, I mean yeah, yeah. That sounds like fun. Going to Aspen, it sounds good."

"Excellent. I'll get my mom to call yours."

This fantasy ends when Mom gets off the phone that evening and huddles with Robert. The Royal *we* appears. We acknowledge I'm doing better, emotionally, and that I'm trying to bring up my grades. We admit that going from a public to a private school can be hard. We hint that if David had been a more frequent visitor to the house and if Robert knew his parents (like he knows Jake's, go figure), that we might begin to consider it. But *we're absolutely certain* that we have priorities for winter break that don't include travel with a boy we barely know.

"So does that all make sense?" Mom asks.

"Yeah, it's fine." I can't tell if I'm mad or relieved. I do, however, smile.

"We just want to do what's best for you," Robert adds.

"I know." Disappearing would be a good thing at this point.

"Hey, I got a question," Michael says, coming around the corner with a bagel in his hand. He plops down on the couch next to me. "What would you say if a girl asked me?"

"That's a little different," Robert explains.

"Oh." He takes a bite and finishes his comment with his mouth full. "Okay. Why?"

"Well, for one thing, Katie's younger than you are, and secondly—she's a girl."

"But his family's going to be there."

I continue to be amazed by this new brother I've gotten.

"Michael . . ." Mom's wearing her enough-now expression.

"No, really, why can't she go? It's just a week, adults are present, he's a good guy, and she'll have plenty of time for homework."

Robert sighs and throws the Look at my mom.

"Katie is in danger of flunking geometry, Michael," Mom says. "And that's the bottom line."

Michael heads for the stairs. "The *bottom line* is you don't want her to grow up." He shrugs at me as he leaves the room. "Sorry, Skates . . . I tried."

No worries. Two hours of vectors and trapezoids effectively blunt all disappointment by numbing my brain to outside stimuli. Until there's an instant message from "Hamlet99."

I know immediately that it's David.

hamlet99: i'm bummed you can't go
kt13: me, too. sry
hamlet99: yeah.
kt13: maybe u cn take somebody else?
hamlet99: hm.
hamlet99: maybe.
hamlet99: NOT!
hamlet99: u there
kt13: yeah
hamlet99: feeling stupid now
kt13: why
hamlet99: um, no words
kt13: me 2
hamlet99: easier when ur acting
kt13: lines are gd

hamlet99: i'm going to tell him maggie

kt13: tell me first

hamlet99: i really like you

hamlet99: not just friend-like

hamlet99: uh . . . u there?

kt13: yeah

hamlet99: i actually said that

kt13: same

hamlet99: really

kt13: yeah

hamlet99: whoa

kt13: yeah

hamlet99: wanna go see a movie or something when i get back?

FOURTEEN

In real life there's no such thing as geometry. Not when I have the boyfriend I always wanted: an OMG-he's-cute, older-guy boyfriend who loves theater, does not act stupidly jocklike or fixate on his sex drive—at least that I've seen *yet* (smile, giggle, blush)—a boyfriend who hangs out with me, calls on the phone and, best of all . . . *really* likes me.

Me, Katie!

We go back to school in January, after the most incredible four days of my entire life (excluding of course, New Year's Eve, when my mother said "No way" to the party David's sister was having). In those four days David has taken me to dinner *and* to a movie *and* to a play at the Geffen, *and* we walked around the Santa Monica Promenade *holding hands*.

I have magically morphed to my True Self, the one I sensed but couldn't find, the one that *fits*. I'm funny; I have words (well, most all the time); I can (almost) throw Stacey's bad moods right back at her; I like my family and Robert; I meet David's sister, Casey—we like each other; he meets Michael—and *they* like each other. Corny love songs make sense. My brother can call me "Skates" whenever he wants. And last, but certainly not least, I'm barely—but truly—passing geometry.

Which means—in real life—I can work on the musical that Tess will start directing next week. The one David happens to be in. The one Stacey did *not* get a lead in, much to everyone's surprise. And when we're not in rehearsal, David and I can go out. Which turns out to be nothing like I ever imagined. Going out with David means we talk. About everything—politics, school, stupid people, even religion. David believes in reincarnation. He thinks souls decide things in between lives, and know before they come back each time how long they're going to live.

"It's like you make yourself a promise," he explains one afternoon. We're sitting across from each other on the greenroom couch, waiting for rehearsal to start. His left leg is pressing against mine, and I have a hard time concentrating on what he's saying. "You know, like maybe I decide I need to be responsible for my actions, so I choose a life situation that'll give me chances to do that. Make sense?"

"Um, that would be . . . not a bit."

He laughs. *(I make him laugh!)* "Okay. Imagine that in a past life I was your basic Jake-type, irresponsible and stupid, and say I was high one day and hit some old lady crossing the street. And nothing happened to me because my parents got me out of it. This time around, my soul decides I need to learn about consequences, so I choose to come back disabled or get hurt in a war or something. Voilà. I understand consequences."

"What about the old lady?"

"She chose too. She's working something out."

"Ah. Very convenient." I've gotten over the leg; now I can't stop staring at his eyes.

"Or complicated," he adds.

"What if you screw up again?"

"I keep coming back until I figure it out."

"But how do you know what you're supposed to do when you're here?"

"You don't. That's the challenge."

"Uh-huh." I drop my voice to a whisper. "Why do you think Stacey chose to come back an asshole?"

I catch his smile and miss his answer as Tess pokes her head in the door and motions us to join her. He takes my hand and we head out to the stage. I'm not sure how much I believe David's philosophy, but right about now, does it matter? I'm in a theater. Actors are working through a play. I'm scribbling notes for an amazing director and sucking in that peculiar but intoxicating theater smell—years of sawdust and paint and artists and rented costumes, makeup and excitement and lights. I can feel the warmth being chilled as the ancient AC unit grumbles away under the lines the actors are reading. Behind me the tech director is hanging lights.

It all fits. Even me.

I smile and Tess glances over and smiles back. She thinks I'm pleased because David's just done a very funny bit. She has no clue that Wise Magic Girl is sitting next to her, bathed in an aura of love for every single person in this theater—yeah, even Stacey.

FIFTEEN

"Tell me about Daddy." In our newfound sibling tolerance, I'm lounging with Michael on the balcony of his bedroom. It's a chilly and beautiful February evening; the wind has sent most of the smog scurrying out over the ocean. No doubt the dolphins are gearing up for a protest.

I'm pretending to do homework.

Michael's feeding his face.

"That's random," he says, stuffing in a meatball. My brother does not subscribe to holistic living practices.

"Well, I can't exactly ask Mom, can I?"

"Why do you have to ask at all? You knew him."

"Hardly."

"Skates, you were his favorite."

"Yeah, right, Mister I-do-everything-with-my-dad."

"Uh-huh. Which dad was that?"

"Come on. You were always together."

"Oh yeah, right. You must mean my fantasy father. The one I didn't have."

"How can you say I was his favorite?"

"'It wasn't me.'" He sings it.

"I barely remember him."

He sighs. "Trust me, Skates, you were *it*. He loved the hell outa you."

I have to sit with that for a second. He offers me a hunk of sourdough and asks, "Why is this coming up now?"

"Well, David was talking about reincarnation and—"

"Shit. You believe that crap?"

"It could be true."

"Mm-hmm, and I'm Jack Black."

"All right, so what do you believe?"

"You're born, you fuck up, you die, and the worms have a party. End of story."

"I like David's theory better."

"You just like David."

"Yeah, I do." I start grinning and can't stop.

Michael gets up and closes his bedroom door, then rejoins me on the balcony.

"So do you guys want to come up to San Francisco with me and Casey over break?"

"Excuse me?"

"I'm meeting Steve and his girlfriend in the city. You and David could come too, if you want to."

"Right. Like Mom will let me."

"She will if she thinks it's just you and me, going to see our old friends."

"I don't have any old friends."

"Okay, this is too hard. You don't want to go, just say it."

"I want to go."

"Then stop arguing so much."

"Fine. What do I do?"

"Let me handle it. I'm gonna make it so *Mom* suggests you go, to keep an eye on me."

"And you think that'll work?"

"You have way too much to learn about parents."

SIXTEEN

Closing night we prove the theory that the brains of fifteen-to-eighteen-year-olds exercise *no* judgment at all. Props materialize in the wrong scenes. Doorknobs disappear. The sound of the first act gunshot goes two beats *after* the actor "fires" the gun. David's "dinner" onstage has been laced with peanut butter, so he plays the entire scene with his tongue sticking to the roof of his mouth. The girl who unzips Stacey's costume for her speed change doesn't show. And pasted into the book the two romantic leads ponder at the end of the first act is a full frontal of a hot guy from *Playgirl*.

It sucks. You should never sabotage a show and Tess will no doubt maim whoever's behind it. But—I have never laughed so hard in my entire life.

After curtain call and flowers, the migration begins. The cast party is in the "Pope-head Room" at Buca di Beppo's, and Stacey's parents are footing the bill. This appeals to me about as much as dental surgery—but I can't think of any excuse that doesn't carry Extreme Negative Social Ramification. A brief reprieve occurs when Tess blocks the theater door.

"Closing night cleanup, babies. When it's *all* done, you can *all* go," she announces.

"My part's clean," says Gabe.

"Then strike the chairs." Tess holds up her hand to the next protest. "What part of 'all done' do I need to explain?"

"The restaurant won't hold the tables past eleven fifteen," Stacey protests.

"Work faster."

"We'll clean up," David interrupts, indicating himself and me. My brilliant boy—why didn't I think of that? We get to be heroes; they get to leave. Tess heads for her office to finish up, and David and I begin by stacking the chairs.

"You know there's a ghost in here," he stage-whispers.

"There is not."

"Yeah, there is. This girl saw him a few years ago. Right there, behind you. Scared the shit out of her."

"You're carrying this other world thing a bit too far, my friend," I warn him, glancing over my shoulder.

"He was a cop. He murdered a migrant worker back when this was a police garage. That's why he has to stay around." His voice is getting creepy.

"Stop it." Chairs done, I start picking up props and the other random junk around the set.

"It's true. There's certain places a video camera won't work. That's one way you know for sure. Oh, and the security guy told me that when he hears music playing in here, like in the early early morning, there's never anyone inside. Even Tess says that—"

"Stop! You're freaking me out." I grab the last thing I see—a backpack someone's shoved under the platform upstage left. He doesn't answer. I look around and I don't see him.

"David?"

Suddenly the fluorescents go out. I take a huge, fast, deep breath. "David. Quit playing around." Still no answer. "I mean it—this isn't funny." I start trying to find my way to the wall where the fluorescent switch is, and bump my shin on a platform. Hard.

"Shit!" I lose my balance and topple forward to my knees, onto the platform. The backpack I'm carrying goes flying; I can hear books sliding out. The fluorescent lights turn on.

"Are you okay?" David suppresses a chuckle.

"Perfect, thanks. I'm just bleeding here." I sit down to examine my scratch.

"Poor baby." He barely manages not to laugh as he sits down beside me.

"Asshole."

"Oooh, ow. I was just playing."

"You turned out the frickin' lights."

"And you made a frickin' mess."

I look at the junk that spilled over the platform. The sequined makeup bag is way too familiar. "Oh fine, it's Stacey's stuff."

David clutches his hands and peers nervously around the theater. "Oh God. Not Stacey! We better run!" *I am totally in love with this guy.* One by one he tosses her books, like basketballs, into the backpack. "Uh-oh." He holds up a small, elegant journal, raises his eyebrows, and asks, "We can't, right?"

"Right."

"Because *she* would never read something that didn't belong to her." With a wink, he drops it into the pocket of his jacket and we finish in silence, conspirators.

"Are you okay here alone?" David asks Tess when we're ready to go. He's doing his Nice Guy act.

"Yes, I am, thank you," Tess says, no trace of teacher or director—just another person.

SEVENTEEN

We decide we'll only read the pages where we see our names. Then we'll tell Tess we forgot something and I'll pretend to look for it while David slips the journal into the backpack. Stacey'll find it Monday. No one gets hurt and it's no big deal, so why is my heart pounding?

"Jump to the middle?" David asks. "Or do you think we'll be on the very first page?"

"We will definitely *not* be on the first page."

We settle in to the backseat of his car, cuddling, and scan the book for our names.

"God, she's got terrible handwriting," I say. We run our eyes down each page and David flips to the next one every five seconds or so. She uses initials mostly, but no K's or D's show up.

"Wait a minute, hold on," David says, and takes the book away from me. He reads by himself as I poke him with my finger.

"No fair, man," I protest.

"No, no . . . shhh. Just a sec."

"Come on, we're supposed to—"

"Katie, just a sec, okay?" His tone is just this side of Not Very Nice. He sighs and hands me the journal. It's all way too dramatic and I make a face at him before I start to read.

October 17—sometime around midnight
Yeah, well, that was fun—especially the part where I got my stomach pumped—what a rush. I lost three pounds and my mother is furious. I should do this more often.

"That was the party?" I ask.
  "Yep. Keep reading."

October 18
He says he's going to sue the school. Typical. If it's not about him, it's not about anything. L says I need to say something. I say she needs to realize I can handle it. Besides, I'm outa here in three more months and he has to pay for my college. All of it.

October 27
Oh my God. My mother wants to get me a shrink—so I can WORK ON LETTING GO OF MY FANTASIES ABOUT MY STEPFATHER! How funny is that? I can't wait to tell L.

Halloween
Grounded. Shit.

November 3
Opening night was amazing except for the scene after where my mother told me that I'd better concentrate on my acting and stop messing up her life. If I do anything else

*stupid, I'm going to boarding school and pay for my own
damn college. Fuck her. Oh sorry. Everyone already has.*

"Okay, well, call me blond, but what are you seeing besides your
basic dysfunctional family?" He takes the book, flips pages, and
hands it back.

*Christmas to New Years
Little benefits—he got me the coat I wanted. Told me not to
show Mom. Maybe he should tell her to stop snooping in
my stuff. God bless L and J for getting me out of the house
most of break. And for the hot guy I met in Aspen.*

*January 7
One month, three weeks, one day, and seven hours but
who's counting. Maybe he thinks Mom knows something.
Maybe she does.*

*January 29
Shit shit shit shit. He caught me. I forgot it was Mom's
conference in San Diego. When did I get this stupid? By
the time I realized she was gone, he was already drinking
and it was too late to get out of the house. I hate him more
than is humanly possible.*

I close the book and we stare at each other. David speaks first.
"You think. . . ?"
"I don't know. It could be."
"Check this out." He flips to a new page.

*March 4
In my dreams, I saw off his dick, slowly, with a dull, rusty*

64

blade. Then I stick it in his mouth, shove it down, and he dies. I laugh.

"That was a few days ago." He sighs. "What do we do?"

"There's nothing we can do," I say. "Right? Is there?"

"Well, we sure as hell can't put it back and pretend we never saw it. She's obviously in trouble."

"Then she should tell someone."

"I think we should give it to Tess."

"David, if Stacey finds out—"

"It doesn't matter."

"She already hates me."

"This isn't about you. I think we have to tell."

Tess reads the page we show her and doesn't ask how we got the book. She thanks us and tells us to go on home and that she'll take care of things. She also tells us she's going to say she found it herself. She asks us not to discuss it anymore, because that could make it harder on Stacey.

As we close the door, she begins to dial the phone.

EIGHTEEN

What's your soul supposed to learn when you come back and molest a kid? I can't sleep because I can't get Stacey out of my mind. Everything about her takes on a different meaning—a subtext I didn't even consider. Of course she's arrogant and aloof. Of course she drinks and takes drugs and doesn't care who she sleeps with—it all makes sense.

I think back to that Saturday rehearsal day when she was late and try to remember what her stepdad looks like. I can't. He's too ordinary; he blends in with all the other dads. Absolutely nothing about him would make you look twice.

Monday I keep an eye out for Stacey, but don't see her or her car parked in the alley. Tuesday's the same. Wednesday I get behind Layla at snack, in line for the food truck. "So where's your other half?" I inquire, with definite Mack Truck subtlety.

"College trip." It seems she freezes up a bit after that, but I can't tell for sure.

David sees Stacey drive up on Friday, a few minutes after snack ends. He text-messages me in class. At lunch we watch her and Layla drive away, just like always.

"Maybe we were wrong," David says.

"Maybe."

After school, on my way to a meeting with Tess, I hear someone stomp in through the other entrance.

"Hi, Stace." Tess's voice.

I freeze, then slowly crack open the greenroom door so I can hear.

"You found my backpack."

"There. On the couch."

No voices for a second. I imagine Stacey opening and rummaging through it.

"Where's my journal?"

"You know where it is."

Another silence.

"I thought we were friends, Tess."

"This has nothing to do with our relationship."

"You called the police. They came to my house."

"I called the Children's Protective Agency, Stacey. *They* called the police."

"Why couldn't you just call me?"

"I'm required by law to report any suspected abuse."

"Yeah, well, are you *required by law* to snoop through my stuff?"

I realize I'm holding my breath.

"You left it in the theater. I had to find out who it belonged to. Your wallet isn't in there and you don't have your name on any of your textbooks. So I looked in your journal."

"I don't believe you." This time, a short silence. "Anyway, you totally overreacted. That was all character work."

"I don't think so."

"Yep. So you screwed up my week for nothing."

"I read the whole journal, Stacey. It's pretty clear what's been going on, and—"

"Nothing's been going on, so fuck it, okay? Let it go. Nothing happened. Except I'm on restriction—thanks to you. And stay out of my stuff, or my mom will call her lawyer."

Meanwhile, *my* mom's going for Mother of the Year. I get to stay out an hour later on school nights and until two on the weekend—if homework's done and I'm with "Davy." She loves the boy. She tells Michael *he* should act more like him. Then she asks me if I'll go with Michael to Santa Rosa on spring break; she doesn't want him driving by himself. She even offers to call Ginny's mom to see about a visit, but I manage to say we had a little fight and I'd rather stay with Michael at Steve's.

"Set it up however you like, honey. You've earned it. And thank you." That almost gets me. And when I realize how completely both David and Michael are playing her, I have a brief moment of guilt. It passes. What people don't know can't hurt them.

I watch Stacey the entire next week, but nothing's different. She's still Arrogant Asshole Girl, though I have to admit she's not as rude to me as usual. Probably because I am Girl with Boy now, a generally Status-Raising Condition.

I go online and find out more about child abuse than I ever wanted to know.

"This could affect her entire life," I tell David as we're driving to school one day. "She is never going to be the same."

"Katie," David replies, patient as ever, "does the word *obsession* mean anything?"

"I'm not obsessed—I just don't get it. Why didn't she say something? Tess would help her. She could get the asshole arrested."

"Maybe she didn't want to."

"That doesn't make sense."

"You're going off again."

"Sorry. But she's not the kind of girl who would let this happen."

"What kind of girl would?"

NINETEEN

"It's our week now, okay?"

I'm down with that. I'm down with switching cars with David's sister so she can ride with Michael and I can be with David. And with my mom not knowing what I'm doing.

"No school, no show stuff, and definitely no Stacey," David instructs as I slide in his car. I nod, but I don't think I'm really all here. Because we're on our way to San Francisco.

We get in around two. I have the keys, since Michael and Casey are going pick up his friends. We have to park a few blocks away and lug our suitcases over. David keeps checking over his shoulder.

"What are you looking for?" I want to know.

"Nothing. Just . . . looking." Two burly bald guys saunter past, and he tenses.

"David, are you scared?" I ask and get his don't-be-ridiculous expression—but he is, I can tell. He thinks we're going to get mugged. When we finally get inside, he relaxes. So do I—the house is perfect, a funky old Victorian, the essence of San Francisco.

"Is this where you and Michael grew up?" he asks, perching on the window seat to peer outside.

"No, it belongs to a friend who's in Mexico. She goes to SF State." He finishes checking, and I can tell he's relieved. "Okay, where to for lunch?" He shakes his car keys and I work to keep from laughing; he's so brave now. "Someplace good—I'm starving."

"Fisherman's Wharf. And we're taking the streetcar." I grab his hand on the way out. "Don't worry, I'll protect you."

"See him?" I point to the beefy, sweaty, hairy guy in a wife-beater, cooking up the lobsters in an outdoor pot. We're at the best outdoor fish place in town. I *know* San Francisco. David loved the streetcar and the cable car. Now he's slurping up chowder in a bread bowl and loving that, too. "Right before they bake that bread, he takes the loaf and swipes it under each arm. That's what gives it the tang."

David stops mid-bite and I bust out laughing. After, we check out Pier 39 and watch the seals push each other off the rocks. We visit tourist shops, have a blue-screen video shot of us "flying" a magic carpet over the Bay, and make reservations to tour Alcatraz Prison the next day. We eat a late dinner at a seafood bar called Swann's on Polk Street, and David proceeds to share the secret of sourdough with the guy behind the counter. I call Michael and we coordinate the nightly check-in. He has me do it since Mom's less likely to worry if I tell her he's out with Steve.

Then we go "home" and it doesn't take me but ten minutes to turn schizo. I plunge into my strange alternate reality—and marvel as Stupid Kate heads up to a bedroom with a boy! Fog seeps into my head. I wanted to be with him, I really did—right up to *now*, when it's actually going to happen. *Now* I don't know what the hell I want.

The bed's a queen mattress on the floor, by a bay window. Clean sheets are folded on top, and we put them on together. David rambles about the day; I manage to slow the flow of the fog-turned-mush as it oozes relentlessly in search of my brain.

"I'll change first, all right?" he says, pointing to the bathroom. I stare blankly in his direction, no doubt giving Subtle Clues that I'm a bit flustered. He smiles, takes my hands and kisses each one. "We're just going to sleep, Katie. Okay? Wearing clothes." I nod. At least I think I do.

"I'll sleep on the floor if you want me to, but I'd actually rather hold you. All right?"

Stupid Kate blinks but doesn't speak.

"Not because I don't want to be with you. I just don't think it's time yet." He smiles. "I mean, I'm perfectly willing to change my mind if you want me to. Do you?" He kisses me on the forehead. Fog has cleared completely.

TWENTY

Right. Sleep. When the guy you are *definitely* falling in love with is right there, in bed next to you? Yes, and I can move objects with my mind, too.

I turn on my side and watch him sleep. When his mouth drops open and he starts to snore, I morph to Silly Child at Sleepover; I cannot stop giggling. He doesn't budge. I tickle his nose to see what he'll do. He snorts a bit and turns over, then farts—a little tiny one. I'm giddy trying not to laugh out loud. When I finally get myself under control, I settle in, back to back, loving how the bulk of him makes me feel safe. There won't be bad dreams tonight.

I'm not aware of dropping off to sleep—the next thing I know, sunlight's streaming in through the blinds.

I wake first and nuzzle up close; David turns away and pulls the covers over his head. I snuggle again—he snarls. I say, "Good morning," he mumbles something nasty, sits up, and scratches himself. I go to the bathroom to get dressed and come out prepared to ignore him. Except he's standing in the middle of the room like a little lost boy—with the front of his boxers sticking straight out. I can't help laughing! He grunts as he slams the bathroom door.

We spend the week doing everything tourists are supposed to. We see Alcatraz. We walk over the Golden Gate Bridge and go down into Sausalito. We explore Stanford University, where David's dad went to school. We have dinner at the Top of the Mark. We drive up the coast, all the way to Point Reyes. I call my mom every night and start to catch on to how easy it is to fool a parent.

We start our last day in the Haight-Ashbury for breakfast, trek over to the zoo to ride the merry-go-round, and then rent a rowboat in Golden Gate Park. We end up that night on the San Francisco Beach, huddling for warmth and watching the frothy surf pound on the sand. I cannot ever, in my entire life, remember having this much fun. Back at the house Michael orders dinner for all of us, and before we know it, David and I are alone in our little room.

"This is where I wish I had a script."

My insides turn to water—his tone leaves little doubt about his intentions. I smile the Stupid Kate smile because I know he's trying to figure out how to end this relationship. What perfect timing—we're packing, it's our last night in San Francisco, and I'm riding home tomorrow with Michael.

"I love you, Katie."

I stare. I blink. And need I mention? Smile.

"Um . . . your line?" he says with an impish grin.

Guess what.

"Katie? You probably need to say *something*."

"Um, yeah. . . . Wow."

"Okay, if you could be just a little more specific? Do you

mean 'wow-what-an-asshole' or 'wow-I-love-you-too'?"

"The second one."

"Yeah?"

"Yeah."

He kisses me. I can almost not stand it.

"I love you." He says it again.

"I love you, too." I blush at the words. My thoughts zip about like guppies, but one stands out—I need to *be here* now, completely. I need this experience to be mine, no fog, no mush. David puts a hand on each side of my face.

"You are so pretty."

This is absolutely the most perfect thing that could happen. We manage not to trip over my shoes as we somehow get to the bed, lips locked the whole way. He runs his hand up my arm and over my breast so lightly I barely—and yet *completely*—feel it. He doesn't linger there but puts one hand behind me and gently lifts me toward him so that when he lies down, he can pull me on top.

He kisses me again. I can feel the hardness of him pressing into my hip. He breathes faster. His hand clamps down behind my head and even though he's not hurting me, all of a sudden—

I don't like it. I want him to stop.

I squirm but he doesn't notice; he holds me tighter. I don't understand what's happening to me—the panic simmering inside is way out of proportion. This is David. We're in love. This is what I want.

I manage to get us to roll side by side so I can catch my breath. He smiles, and his voice is like sweet chocolate.

"Sorry, I guess I better slow down, huh?"

When I nod, he moves back a few inches and takes a long, deep sigh.

"Do you *know* how hard this week has been? No pun intended."

I don't trust my voice; I shake my head and smile.

"I'm lucky I got to sleep at all." I think of him snoring and relax a little. He pushes my hair back out of my eyes and kisses my forehead and then my nose. Then he cups my head again and gently guides me toward him. As we kiss, he holds me close. This time we're lying on the bed, facing each other. I feel my body responding to him, wanting him, but panic bubbles up again. I start to breathe really fast.

"I know," he says, with a twinkle in his eye. "Look what you do to me."

He takes my hand and moves it onto the front of him. Holds it there. I freeze. Literally. When he kisses me, I can't move. I'm terrified, and I can't tell him. I want to run away, but I'm not connected to my self anymore. I realize I have no control of my body.

I see David—

I know where I am—

I am aware of the noises in the street and music playing from downstairs—

But I am no longer here.

"Katie?" His voice is soft. "Hey—" He shifts his body and peers into my eyes. "Are you okay?"

The most I can do is turn my eyes to his.

"Oh, baby, you're scared. Don't be scared."

I get to take a breath. It comes out hard.

"Honey, we can stop. It's okay. You want to stop?"

I don't know if I nod. I want to; maybe I do. He smiles. "Hey. I love you." He touches my face. "I can't even tell you how much. It's too strange."

Now I'm starting to cry, little sneaky tears, the ones that leak out whether you want them to or not.

"Katie, don't cry. Nothing to cry about. We don't need to do this now."

"I'm sorry," I manage to say.

"It's okay, it's okay. It's my fault for going too fast. I love you." He takes my chin in his hand and lifts my eyes up to his. "Got that? I—love—you." He glances down and makes a face. "Yeah. Okay. Be right back."

He goes into the bathroom. I sit up and stare out the window.

I don't know what I'm thinking.

I don't know what I feel.

Everything is whirling about way too fast, and I don't seem able to order it in any way that makes sense.

I concentrate on breathing.

I focus on the night outside the window.

I feel I should do something, but don't know what it is.

TWENTY-ONE

"Cat got your tongue?" Michael asks. We're in the jeep, on the 580 toward Sacramento. David and Casey are on their way to Lake Tahoe to meet up with their parents. They have a house there, too.

"Tired."

"You and David didn't sleep too much, huh?" He's wearing his Dumb Jock face, and it makes my stomach twinge.

"It's not like that."

A pause—he loses the smile. "Sorry, Skates." Does he actually *hear* the tone of my voice? "You want to talk about it?"

Magic words. Because yes, I want to talk about it—if only I knew just what the hell *it* was. I sigh. I shrug. He waits a few more minutes before speaking.

"Did David do something? Because, if he did . . ."

"No, not at all. David is amazing." I shrug again and grin at my brother's protectiveness. "I'm fine. Just . . . shit, I don't know. Sometimes I just can't figure me out."

"Ah, yes. Welcome to *my* world."

We make the turn from the 580 to the 5. Nothing but farm-
land on either side now, broken up by rest area truck stops,
Denny's-type restaurants, and gas stations. Oh, and the slaugh-
terhouse. What looks like a million black and white cows stand
placidly packed together on at least five miles of rolling hills. The
smell is horrific. The realization that all those living beings are
waiting to be food makes me ill.

"I'd be fine if I never saw this," Michael comments. "I like to
think my steaks come from stores."

"Yeah, me too."

It'll still be hours before we hit the mountains, and then
another two hours or more to LA. Michael and I both settle
back. We don't talk for a long time, but the silence between us
is easy and nice.

"Hey, Skates, I have a question for you."

"Okay."

"When did you change?"

I chuckle at him. "I could ask you the same thing."

"Hey, I'm the same as I ever was. You're the one went from
shy to radical."

"Maybe I always was radical, and you just didn't know it."

"No, you weren't."

"Well, at least I wasn't a butthead all my life."

"Oh, oh . . . I was?"

"You could teach a class."

"Thanks very much."

"It's okay, you're better now."

"Oh, good to know." He glares at me, then smiles, and we
lapse back into stillness. I'm glad he notices how different I am.
I'm glad that he likes me.

My mind wanders through the changes this year, unexpected
and otherwise. Nothing's in chronological order; David floats in

and out, then Stacey, my old best friend, Ginny, Tess and the plays, my mom and Robert, Michael and Casey, San Francisco, then David again, and last night, briefly, the starkness of Alcatraz, my dad in his hospital bed, the beach—one scenario cross fades with the next in that strangely arbitrary way minds have.

I smile to myself and drift, lulled by the landscape and the rhythm of the reggae jazz CD Michael's playing. Last night's embarrassment tries for center stage, but I banish it to the wings—it doesn't seem important in the greater scheme of things. My brother is becoming my friend, my boyfriend loves me, *and* I'm finally starting to see who I really am.

End of story.

I don't really need to think about anything else.

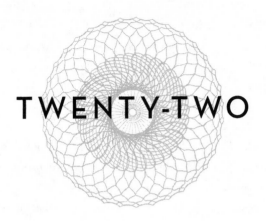

TWENTY-TWO

It sucks how hard I work at geometry, because it never seems to matter. I do not get it. I will never get it. And though I personally do not see the connection between, oh, world peace and my grasp of the isosceles triangle, mine is not a commonly held opinion.

To promote the triangle, the Royal We has returned. "We" are on my case, "for your own good," because "We are looking out for your best interests." Unfortunately, this time I *do* have a life, and a boyfriend, thank you very much. Which they know adds leverage to their side of the Geometry Dilemma. The threat of "no prom" is added to "no phone calls" and "don't even think about seeing Davy until you bring that grade up."

David and I see each other in the car when he picks me up for school and drops me home after. We IM in between homework, and when I don't have to meet with a tutor, we hang out at lunch. It's never long enough and I miss him so much it hurts. Teachers assign five times the amount of homework a normal human can handle, and finals loom, less than eight weeks away.

I have to work to maintain a semblance of balance. I know if I flunk geometry, I'll have to take it this summer. But all I can think about is David.

Until I scrape my arm on a leftover nail in the set we're striking in tech class. "Whoa," I say, when Tess points out the blood on my upper arm. "When did that happen?"

"Omigod. Do not tell me you didn't feel that," Random Annoying Girl pipes up.

"Actually, I didn't. Or you know what, I would've said."

Tess takes my other arm. "Come in the greenroom; we'll get you cleaned up."

The wound ends up looking a lot worse than it actually is, but I definitely should have felt it. Tess fills out an accident report, tells me to have my mom check my tetanus shots, and says nothing more on the subject. She does, however, watch me pretty closely the rest of the hour. I watch myself, too, remembering the blackouts I had in ninth grade. It's time for more "research"—but this has to be live.

"Michael, what do you remember about me, last year?" Our nightly hang is pretty regular these days—especially with both of us on Academic Lockdown—and it's not at all hard to ask this.

"Um, you got pregnant? I don't know. I was a butthead, remember? We weren't talking. Why? Did I miss something?"

"Just that I thought I was schizophrenic." *Okay, said it.*

"Seriously?"

"Yeah."

"How'd you come up with that?"

"Online. I had most of the symptoms."

"Shit. You tell Mom?"

"Of course not. What do you think?" *Second thoughts, but the words keep coming.*

"Damn, did you like hear voices or something?"

"No. I just got sorta disconnected; it was weird. I didn't react to things when they happened; I had really bad dreams; and sometimes I'd be at home or in class or walking and I wouldn't remember how I got there."

"Shit, Skates."

"Yeah." *Way too much information just came out, but I can't seem to stop.* "Basically, I managed okay until it happened in class; I 'came to' and everybody was staring at me. Ms. Zimmerman freaked. She called Mom, and I had to go see the school counselor."

"Why didn't I know this?"

"I don't know. You had your own problems, I suppose. And you weren't around much."

"What'd the counselor say?"

"She thought it was a delayed reaction to Daddy dying." Once these words are out, the air seems to change. We've never really talked about our dad, not alone, and I am no longer comfortable. I feel suddenly sleepy and I notice Michael's mouth starts that little twist. *Shut up, Katie, fix this.* "But it stopped, and then Mom met Robert and we moved here, and so, uh, yeah." *Too late.* He's gone quiet; I've gone quiet. We're not looking at each other.

Awkward, Party of Two. No way can I tell him about wounds I don't feel and freak-outs with the boyfriend.

"Do you know what's really amazing?" Michael says, finally. "I never believed he was going to die."

"I didn't either."

"Yeah?" He tries to smile, but his mouth is too tight. His brows pull together and for a second I'm scared he might start to cry.

"Uh, you want to talk about it?" I know how lame I sound, but it's the best I can come up with.

"I'm okay."

"Michael . . ."

He kinda shakes himself, like a dog with water. "You know I'm moving back, don't you? I'm gonna live with Steve."

The change is too abrupt; it's hard to put my words together. "Why?"

"I hate it here, Skates. I hate the school. I hate the people. I want to get a job and eventually go away someplace to college."

"But Robert said he'd pay—"

"Robert is not my father. I'm going to pay for myself."

"What about Mom's wedding?"

"I'll go after. Maybe July or August. I'm already enrolled in the JC. Mom doesn't know yet, so . . ."

"No problem."

"Sorry, Skates. I really am."

TWENTY-THREE

School is out of control. For the 10-billionth time, I wonder how I'd get through this last semester if I didn't have acting class in the afternoon. I wait all day for these two hours.

"Five minutes . . ." someone calls through the greenroom door.

"Okay," I call back.

I take a huge breath, close my eyes, and visualize a small point of color in my mind. I banish triangles and other academic trivia and concentrate on what's important—getting ready to do this final monologue. This pushes the rest of the world away, and lets me focus, commit to my action, and . . .

Someone's in the room. My eyes fly open—there's a man in the corner! My brain tells me this isn't possible—the door is shut—but there's his reflection in the makeup mirror. I wheel around and I suck in air so I can scream. I wonder why his face is so dark. Then—he's gone.

I'm by myself. But I *saw a man*.

But you can't see things that aren't there.

But I saw a man.

I can't do lines now; I'm shaking too hard. I lean back against the makeup table; what if I see him again? And what the hell do I tell Tess?

"Um, sorry, can't do my monologue now because, well, I memorized it, but there was this guy in the greenroom—except he really wasn't, but I saw him and I'm totally freaked out now, so, uh, yeah."

So when she calls me up, I go. I say all the words and then call, "Scene."

"All right," Tess announces, low and drawn out the way she does when the work's bad and she's trying not to hurt the actor's feelings. "How was that for you?"

"It was okay." I sound pissy.

"Anything you want to work on?"

"Um, no, not really, at least not right now."

"You sure?"

"Yeah. I'm not feeling so good."

"Okay. Let's have you do it again next week, all right? Give some more thought to specifics—who you're talking to, what you want from them, and how you plan to get it. Yeah?"

I nod. Tess is puzzled, but I can't care about that right now. I need to concentrate on how to get out of class before I do something strange.

The man comes back again, two days later. This time I'm home, in my room, getting ready for bed. I've crammed as much geometry into my brain as I can for the quiz we're having tomorrow. I slip under the covers and sigh at how good it is to be lying down. I say a silent prayer that sleep won't erase everything I think I've memorized and reach over to turn off the light.

It's the same exact feeling, except this time I have an idea what to expect. My eyes adjust to the dark and I scan the room. He's over by the window. Even with his face hidden in shadows, there's something about him I recognize, like I've seen him before. I reach slowly for my light and turn it on. He disappears.

There's no going to bed; way too much adrenaline is pumping through my veins. I breathe, but can't relax, even with the light on. None of my usual tricks work. I tiptoe over to my brother's room; his light's out. I traipse down the stairs but make a U-turn at the bottom and end up back in my room. Finally I grab my geometry book and realize it is good for something—maybe I can numb myself enough to sleep.

Finals get closer and teacher tolerance shrinks in direct *opposite* proportion to the swell of student paranoia. Classes accelerate and expand, and there's simply too much noise—in the yard, in the classroom, driving in the car. I'm having a hard time keeping track of what I'm supposed to do. I desperately need to avoid a public display of my recurring hallucination, and yet I can't seem to keep my focus on anything. I start counting—cracks in the pavement, bricks on the wall, the number of lines in the hardwood floor, even the words in my reading assignment. It lets me concentrate on planning the next half hour and perpetuates the pretense that I'm still running my own life.

Which I clearly am not.

In brief rational moments, I give thanks for David's Ivy League college dreams. He has AP bio, trig, Latin IV, Great Books, honors U.S. history—*and SAT II's*—leaving no room to worry about anything else. He doesn't notice I've completely stopped talking; he assumes I'm in the same boat as him.

But my boat has a leak. I've got an oar and I paddle frantically and constantly, but I don't move out of my own tiny circle. I can't see land in any direction; I can't find the horizon; I don't have a clue which way I'm supposed to go. I keep whirling around to try to catch sight of whatever's chasing me, but I never quite see it. Meanwhile, I'm steadily sinking. And it's still five weeks till summer.

I wonder if you know when you're going insane.

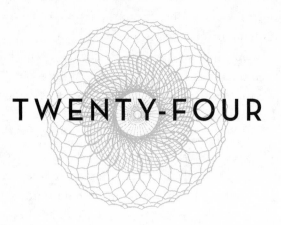

TWENTY-FOUR

I have the dream, but this time it isn't the Monster—it's the scary man, without any face. This time he's not content to skulk in the corner; he comes closer and closer, and I want to run away but something's holding me down. His hands are on me and he lifts me and all of a sudden I realize my eyes are open, and this isn't a dream or a hallucination—

It's a memory.

I see myself as a little girl—skinny, two long honey-blond braids, blue eyes, in Winnie-the-Pooh pajamas, sleeping in my yellow bedroom with the rainbow trim and the large framed picture of Minnie Mouse, in our blue and white house in Santa Rosa. I hear the shushed *slap-slap* of bare feet on the hardwood floor. There's a shadow in the doorway, then a creak and a click as the door is gently shut.

He's in the room.

He's smiling.

I'm afraid.

His voice confuses me: *How's my girl tonight?*

I see the little girl who is me squeeze her eyes tight shut, hoping he'll think she's sleeping and go away. He doesn't. He never does. He comes to the bed and carefully pulls back the covers.

You're a good girl, Skates.

His voice slides to a rough, hoarse, scratchy whisper that doesn't sound at all familiar.

I love you very much.

The little girl who is me keeps her eyes closed.

Don't worry, sweetie.

The hand that slides around the back of the little girl's head is the same one that saved her from the ocean.

I won't hurt you.

The other hand pulls her up and out of bed and he slides in and puts her on top. He holds her tight; she's so small against him. He breathes faster and faster and slides her back and forth. She would scream except his hand is holding her face pressed into his chest, and it's hard to breathe. She would tell him to stop—he *is* hurting her—but her voice is traveling up, into her head, where it will not be found, where no one will ever hear it.

He rolls her to her back and takes her hand and moves it to touch him. She opens her eyes and looks up, but can't see his face anymore. She counts the rainbows on the wallpaper. She stares past him to the large framed picture of Minnie Mouse in her yellow polka-dot dress. She feels herself starting to float up and apart. Minnie reaches out a gloved hand and grabs her arm. The fog drifts in and the danger recedes, like the tide. The little girl who is me is safe. Nothing can hurt a floating child.

I sit up.

For a second or two, I don't recognize my own room; I feel drunk—altered. I look around, half expecting Minnie Mouse and rainbows and finally realize this is now. I'm at Robert's. I concentrate on breathing and look for something to count. There are vertical blinds, but counting them over and over doesn't help.

Because I know.

I don't want to—but I do.

Something happened to me when I was little, something very bad. I don't know details or remember when it started.

I'm not sure when or why it finally stopped.

But I recognize the Monster.

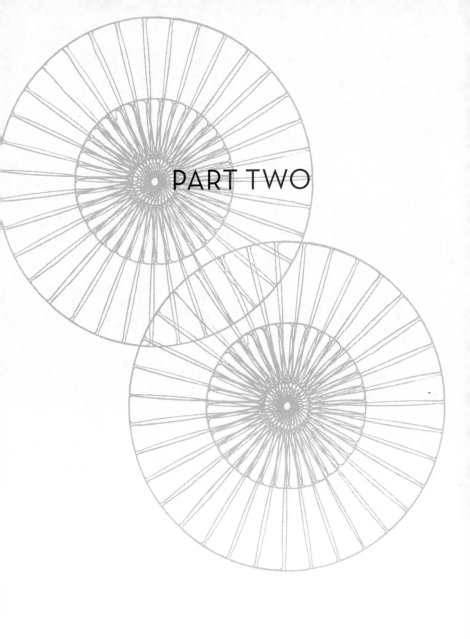

PART TWO

TWENTY-FIVE

Prom is in two weeks, and though David insists he doesn't "expect" anything, he's reserved a hotel suite with a couple of his senior friends.

Which makes me kinda tingle in anticipation.

Which makes me remember San Francisco.

Which makes me angry—because now I have this "memory."

Which absolutely, positively, cannot be true.

Except it is.

Those are my father's eyes I see over me, seconds before I blot them out. That's his hand reaching from the Monster's body. It's his breath soft and warm in my face.

David wants me to come over tonight; his parents aren't going to be home. I'm supposed to call and tell him when to pick me up. Instead, I sit in my room and don't move from the bed. I stare out the window at the sky past the huge oak that owns our backyard. Now that I know, the hallucinations have stopped. *But at what price?*

The man who swept me up in his arms to save me from the ocean, the man Michael says loved me the best and rescued me from everything from scraped knees to little-girl traumas—*how dare I imagine this man could ever hurt me?* He was my daddy. I miss him more than I will ever be able to say. What sick stupid person have I become? *What is wrong with me?!*

But even as I rage, piling argument upon argument in defense of his innocence, his love, his self—I know. Like words to a song I can almost remember and never escape, the melody lurks in my bones.

Mathematicians are immune to essential issues of humanity— even the most desperate personal situation cannot alter a home-work due date. So it matters not to my geometry teacher why I was up until three; only that I didn't finish her assignment. Acting teachers tend to be a little more sensitive, but even Tess doesn't let me get away with two bad monologues.

"We'll talk tomorrow, okay?" she says as I'm leaving class. "When's your free?"

"Third. But I have to meet my geometry tutor."

She smiles. "Well, this will only take a few minutes."

I watch Tess finish up a phone call. She's definitely an older woman—her face full of lines and creases, her hair streaked with gray—but she's also somehow young. Maybe because nothing for her is halfway—she simply doesn't compromise. I want to tell her what I think might have happened to me and ask what the hell to do about it. But when I try the words out in my head, they're awkward and melodramatic and make me sound like I'm in a soap, playing the hysterical teenager who craves attention.

There's also that little issue about the police being called to Stacey's house.

Tess hangs up and peers over her desk. "Okay, baby. What's going on?"

"I am so sorry. I just wasn't prepared."

"I'm not talking about your monologue."

"No?" I give my best stab at innocence.

"No. What's going on with you?"

"Nothing. I'm good." I try my cute kid smile. "It's just school stuff. See, I'm basically flunking—"

"Katie, listen," she interrupts. "The thing about artists is this—it may not always feel like it, but we are *of a whole*. We don't compartmentalize very well. If something's going on in our personal life, it finds a way to be in our art. And something is obviously going on for you." Those eyes of hers burn all the way into my brain. "Is it David?"

"No, no, I swear! I'm just stressed, from school and my mom getting married. . . ."

"All right." She keeps examining me and I finally have to look away. "It's not my business unless you want it to be. And it's totally okay if you don't. But know that you *can*."

"Okay."

She sighs and smiles. "And please figure out what your character wants in that damn scene."

"Got it."

TWENTY-SIX

Tight. Small. Thumbs tucked inside the fingers and fists closed until it hurts. Back rigidly immobile, even my face is polar, the tiny muscles around my eyes refusing to budge, mouth pulled just ever so slightly and stuck. Legs crossed, back of my knee over thigh and again, ankle wrapped around ankle. All the openings clenched, involuntarily? Nothing can get in. But the other reason. Nothing can get out.

"Katie? You okay?" my brother asks.

    "Yeah, end-of-the-year stress, you know."

    "Sure?"

    "Absolutely."

    "Okay, well, I'm here. If you . . . you know."

    "Yeah. Thanks."

Strange how we all have our scripts. Except mine isn't working so well, not that anyone notices. I have plenty of lines, but none that make sense. This scene should have been played years ago, before the subtext got twisted and hidden and I spent all that time thinking I was going crazy.

Which still might be the truth. I am willing to consider all possibilities, and I am doing everything in my power to keep some kind of perspective. Otherwise I could turn out like Stacey—doing drugs, having rampant sex—oh wait, no, I can't. I freak out when my totally wonderful boyfriend holds me.

"I can't wait to have some real time with you!" David says as he drops me off at home after school. His eyes have smudgy dark circles under them from late-night studying. We haven't even had time for IM's or phone calls. "I miss you."

"Me too."

"I love you."

"I love you, too."

Maybe it's all a desperate attempt to blame someone besides myself for that fact that I'm so screwed up. It is clever—create a deep dark secret to account for social ineptitude and a serious inability to fit in, but choose something that can't possibly be proven or disproven, because the "perpetrator" is dead and it happened where nobody else saw.

Besides—if any of this were real—someone else would have known. It was a small house. My bedroom was next to Michael's and just down the hall from our parents'. My mom used to wake up when she heard me going past her room to the bathroom. At the very least she would have noticed that my door was shut. I hated going to bed with the door shut.

"Okay, you really have to tell me the truth."

My mother has her wedding gown on. It's strapless and laces like an elegant corset in the back. "Do I look fat?"

"You look amazing."

"Do I look *old*?"

"You look beautiful."

"Really, truly?"

"Beautiful." And she is.

If something this awful happened, why didn't I say something? Nobody screamed in my family. Nobody got hit. I wasn't scared of my mother. Why didn't I tell her? Unless there was really nothing to tell, because it didn't really happen. Maybe I dreamed it. Maybe I got confused. It's perfectly reasonable that I dreamed the Monster and then my dad came to tuck me in and I made him part of the dream.

Because this is not the kind of experience people forget.

Except I did.

"Kate, honey, when you have a moment, will you stop by my office?" Robert asks as I'm going upstairs to study after dinner. "I'd like to talk to you about something."

"Uh, okay." My stomach starts warming up for tricks.

"It won't take long."

"You mean like, tonight?"

"Yeah. If you can. Thanks. I'll be up till eleven."

The biggest question of all is why?

I was a little girl. Only sick, terrible, nasty men do bad things to little children. My father was not that. My father was a kind man. He loved me. He loved all of us. He would never do anything hurtful, not on purpose. He took care of me and he made me laugh. Even during chemo, when he got so weak he had to stay in bed, he was never cruel, never mean or awful.

And yet . . .

TWENTY-SEVEN

Robert's attention is so completely focused on the computer screen in front of him, he doesn't notice me tapping on his office door, which is cracked open a couple of inches. I watch a minute; he's a different guy when he's not gazing Puppy Eyes at my mom. He actually looks distinguished! I find it bizarre that I barely know this man and in another month, he's going to be my "father."

I push open the door and step inside. He glances over, smiles, and goes back to typing. "One sec, Katie." I stand by the door, willing my stomach to stop turning cartwheels. Why am I nervous again? Maybe because there's nothing in the world we could possibly need to talk about? And it's almost eleven and I have at least two hours of homework left? Just then he shuts his laptop.

"Sorry, I really had to finish that." His eyes look tired. "I appreciate you coming down. Close the door for me?"

Whoa. Stacey's stepdad lands smack dab in the middle of my brain. The door clicks, but I stay standing.

He indicates the couch. "This won't take long."

I perch on the arm. If he even hints at inappropriate, I'm outa here. And I don't plan to be quiet about it. But he just rubs his eyes and settles back a little in his chair.

"I'm going to jump right in, okay? I heard Michael on the phone with his buddy from Santa Rosa. He's planning to move back up there after the wedding."

I blink.

"Do you know about this?" His voice is kind, not at all like someone who wants to interrogate me.

I nod and wish I hadn't; I told Michael I wouldn't tell.

"Do you know why?"

"Uh . . . I think. . . . well, um . . ." *Oh, brilliant.*

"Katie, I promise I won't say anything to your mom or to Michael. I just need to know if I did something."

"No. I don't think so."

"You pretty sure on that?"

"Uh-huh." I take a really close look at Robert and realize for the first time how very hard it must be to love a woman with two teenagers. I kick myself—figuratively, of course—for suspecting him. "He doesn't like LA."

"That makes sense. Thank you." I'm just about ready to stand up when he adds, "And how are you doing?"

"I'm okay."

"End of the year sucks, doesn't it?"

"Pretty much."

"I'm proud of how hard you're working."

"Yeah, well, I still might have to take geometry over the summer."

"So what. That's what summers are for, huh?"

"Actually, I thought they were for swimming."

He laughs, and I find myself liking how his eyes crinkle up. He reminds me a little of Tess. "Robert, why haven't we met

100

your daughters?" I blurt it out. *Way to go, Kate, one step forward and five back.*

"That's direct."

"I'm sorry. Forget it, it's not my business."

"Actually, it probably is." He shrugs. "You haven't met them because they've chosen not to be part of my life." His face sags a little. "I can't say I blame them. I wasn't much of a dad. My priorities were definitely skewed. We had a great life—but I was never around."

"Oh."

"The divorce wasn't friendly." He looks embarrassed now and I wish I'd kept my big mouth shut. He reaches across his desk and picks up a picture of two teenage girls. I stand to take it. "That's my girls—Jan and Elizabeth. Of course, that's a while ago."

The girls are in soccer uniforms that say "Bentley Evans Prep" on the front. I suddenly realize why I was able to get in there at the last minute.

"Maybe if they knew you were getting married. . . ?"

"They do. But your mom's only forty, and they're thirty-two and thirty-four. They're invited. Lisa is too, their mom. But I doubt they'll come."

"Oh." I hand him back the photo, then settle into the chair next to his desk.

"Bonnie knows all this. She understands."

"Oh. Good."

"She's an amazing woman."

"Yeah, I guess she is."

"She's changed my life."

I don't know what to say, so I smile.

"It must have been hard on you all when Tom died."

"Did you know my dad?"

"No, but I feel like I did. Your mom's talked a lot about him.

He sounds like a wonderful man."

Okay, explain this: I have to blink to keep from crying. Robert stands and reaches across the desk to touch my arm lightly, briefly, then settles back. His voice is gentle.

"I'm sorry, Katie. I shouldn't have said anything. I know you loved him very much."

"No, it's okay." I smile. Again. Of course.

"Listen, I'm not trying to take his place, all right? Because no one could. But—" He grins, in a mischievous way. "I would like to do a couple of dad things. If it's all right with you."

I shrug; I'm not quite sure what he means.

He winks and reaches for his wallet. "How about we start with Prom. You're going with your boyfriend, right?"

I realize he doesn't miss much. "Yeah."

"Got a dress yet?"

"No, I haven't had time to think about it."

"Good. Dad thing number one." He hands me a silver credit card. "No limit, whatever you want. I mean that. Dress, shoes, hair, jewelry . . . everything. My treat."

I fall asleep that night around two, trying to figure out what exactly happened, why I feel calm now instead of frantic. My homework isn't finished and nothing's solved, but something fundamental seems to have shifted and settled, like the floor of a house after a small earthquake.

TWENTY-EIGHT

Only eight days till Prom, and either I tell David I've changed my mind or I go and buy a damn dress. But where the hell do you find such a thing, and what is it supposed to look like? Being your basic jeans and a T-shirt girl, I can't recall the last time I wore anything resembling "fancy."

I ask my mother for help and get the lecture about waiting until the last minute and can't I see she's just a little tied up right now planning her wedding? Yes, of course I can see this, but I press on anyway: "Maybe I could wear the dress you got me for the wedding?" I smile hopefully—I really like it and then I wouldn't have to shop. She rolls her eyes and flounces out of the room, announcing as she goes that this dress costs more than three months' rent on the blue and white house.

Which apparently is infinitely more significant than the fragile psyche of her kid. Obviously she doesn't hear *my* angst; Prom is now, the wedding is whenever, and having the Perfect Dress has unexpectedly become my Most Pressing Issue. Pretty much all I can worry about right now.

Michael takes pity on me. After explaining—*in graphic older-brother language*—the circumstances under which he'd even *consider* shopping with me, he suggests I call David's sister, Casey. She goes to Harvard-Westlake, and if anyone knows how to shop, it would be her. I do, she agrees, and we arrange to go the next day, the very last Saturday before Prom. Casey brings a friend, Kira. They ask a bunch of questions about color, style, etc.—do I want vintage or couture or do I have my own ideas? Stupid Kate smiles. They ask me what David will be wearing— I hold palms up and smile bigger. Finally they ask, "Okay, do you have a budget?" and I present Robert's platinum Visa. One out of three. Phew. I'll settle. Ten points for the stepdad.

Casey exchanges a fairly wicked glance with Kira.

"I know," Kira agrees. "With *that* body . . ."

I can only hope she means something good.

Casey winks at me. "This is going to be fun."

We arrive at Fendi in Beverly Hills and a valet parks our car. Inside I smile at the salesgirl, who looks exactly like Zooey Deschanel in *The Good Girl*; she sighs as if I've seriously interrupted her day. As Casey and Kira flit through the racks and pull out this swirly lovely thing and that flimsy sexy thing, I check out a T-shirt that's pretty cute, wondering if there's such a thing as casual at a prom. I glance at the tag and have to look again. $313!

"Katie," Kira commands, and hands me a pair of high heels they've snagged from Zooey Girl. Casey follows with five dresses and points me toward the changing room. Which is pretty much the size of my bedroom in Santa Rosa.

The first two—not so good—I wouldn't be seen in public in either one. The third is killer: black, fitted, simple, and elegant, with an extremely low back. Suddenly being Skinny with No Tits works. I glance at the tag and once my heart starts again, I choose to ignore it. Robert said anything I want. Good for me.

When I come out to show the girls, they actually jump to their feet. Even Zooey Girl likes it.

"Oh yeah," says Casey, nodding. "Oh very yeah."

Kira sweeps my hair up off my shoulders, and we all three admire how I look. Zooey Girl brings over a necklace and earrings. They're perfect.

"My brother won't have a chance," Casey says. "We'll take it," she tells the girl, then quickly looks back at me. "Oh, Katie, sorry. Do you like it?"

Do dogs poop?

We find the perfect shoes and something truly wicked for After Prom, then do a quick stop at Casey's stylist to make an appointment for me to get my hair, nails, and makeup done. The girls fill me in on Proper Prom Protocol, and I finally remember my upbringing and offer to buy them lunch. They opt for mocha Frappuccinos. One drawback. Since the afternoon has been entirely too awesome, the Universe sends us to the very same Starbucks Layla and Stacey happen to be visiting. They're deep into conversation on the patio, sipping chai and smoking cigarettes.

Layla sees me and waves as we walk by. Stacey sends over her usual f-you expression and arrogantly turns away.

"Bitch," Kira mutters, loud enough for them to hear. "You know them?"

"Sort of. They go to my school."

"That's right, they do. I know them too," Kira says. "At least, I know *about* them." She smiles a deadly smile.

"The redhead's a slut," Casey tells me. "She slept with Kira's boyfriend."

I think: No doubt he fought her off. I say: "Wow."

"Yeah, wow." Casey looks at me over her sunglasses. "You're not like good friends or anything, are you?"

"No, we were just in a play together."

"Omigod, that's right!" Casey says. "They were in David's play. They were actually good."

TWENTY-NINE

Prom. Me. Damn.

I had doubts about going to my own prom, and here I am, in *tenth grade*, watching my Beautiful Boyfriend walk up to the door of my Brentwood mansion, dressed like I'm Kate Hudson, feeling pretty much able to conquer the world.

Who knew?

Mom and Robert take 3 billion pictures and finally we get in David's car to rendezvous at someone's house I don't know, with our "limo group," more people I don't know. They're all seniors and not theater kids, giving Stupid Kate her chance to go to Prom too. I begin Kate's Infamous Smiling Silence. David doesn't seem to notice.

More pictures. The limo arrives and Mr. Charming (real name completely unpronounceable), our slick-haired, middle-aged, gangster-looking driver, has us each sign a "no drinking or drugs" agreement. He assures the moms who are there to see us off that he will take good care of us. But a block down, he pulls over and lays out the rules again—not exactly as polite as he was with the moms. The girls in the car assure him we are Good Teenagers and show him we've only brought Arrowhead, in case we get thirsty, and Gatorade—to replenish our systems from all the dancing, since we are all avid dancers. Bottles are opened and reluctantly, as if he thinks we might overpower him and steal the car, he sniffs, sips, and nods. Finally we're on our way.

Do I catch on that the rest of the Arrowhead bottles are filled with vodka? Um, that would be—not a bit—until I see their contents poured into the Gatorade bottles. I glance at David, who grins as he shrugs and offers me a sip. I take one for the sake of company, make a face, and cause everyone in the car to burst into giggles. Except David, he's very patient. He puts his arm around me and gives me a little squeeze.

We arrive at the old Roosevelt Hotel in Hollywood. The combination of my geometry teacher in a red formal gown and my half bottle of "Gatorade" start me giggling. David likes this; he takes my arm and we find a place to sit. As if they were at some overaged dress-up party, people float from table to table, saying nice things. Even Stacey drifts by and mumbles, "Good dress," though I don't think she realizes she's talking to me.

By eleven most of the girls have changed to After Prom outfits and the boys have summoned the limos. I've spoken maybe four words. As we wait for Mr. Charming to make the turn into the hotel driveway, a police car beeps its warning siren, and flashing lights appear on two sides of one of the smaller limos. Jake comes barreling out of the hotel line with a girl I don't know. "Hey!" he hollers. "What the hell's going on here?"

"Step back, please, sir," an officer tells him as another hauls the limo driver out of his seat. As Jake paces, shaking his head, and the dean hovers, the limo driver is given the Walk the Straight Line exam. He fails. We clap and whoop. A tow truck hooks up his limo, he's plopped into the police car, and Jake makes a scene.

The dean threatens to call his parents. Jake says, "Call my lawyer while you're at it," and keeps on with his entitled assholeness until Layla appears and drags him and his date off with her.

Our driver shows up happier and more pleasant than before. Not. "Gatorade" is passed around and we head off to After Prom, at a club called Tyranny, smack in the middle of Hollywood. We show our school ID's at the door and walk through a curtain to the real prom: no adults, unless you count the paid bouncers; spike heels and short skirts instead of elegant gowns; tons of "Gatorade" and from the smell, plenty of pot. People are practically having sex on the dance floor, including one male/male couple locked at the lips. Two people I don't recall ever seeing at school are actually doing it in the corner. At least that's what it looks like—it's too dark to tell for sure.

Four of us grab a table, and a waitress drops off cranberry juice, which David promptly dilutes with "Arrowhead." Jake and his entourage make their entrance, heading past us to the VIP lounge—which they get to occupy since he and Layla "organized" the After Prom.

"At least she could wipe her nose," someone at our table mumbles, nodding toward Jake's girlfriend.

David whispers, "Cocaine," and I wonder how I've managed to live my entire life completely unaware of Real Teen Behavior. I sip some of my Arrowhead-cranberry drink and pretend I can hear the conversation David's having with the guy at the next table. Mostly, though, I watch.

"Check it out," someone says. Five nearly naked senior girls pose in the doorway, in not much more than bras and bands (read: "skirts") around their hips. A boy I don't know is trying to talk to one of them. Turns out she's his ex, and he's way drunk. The date he brought to Prom tries to pull him away; Nearly Naked starts "dancing" with another guy—the ex goes postal and Prom Date bursts into tears. Nearly Naked's friends make fun of her, and Random Guy—not connected to this drama at all—decides to stop in front of our table to share everything he's eaten or drunk this evening.

That's it. We head for the door. We're outside and hailing our limo before the guy even gets off the floor.

THIRTY

Final Prom stop—the Sheraton in Santa Monica. Almost the whole floor is taken up by the seniors from Bentley Evans Prep, and I feel very sorry for anyone that isn't part of the party. People stumble up and down the hallways, ducking in and out of rooms. They have champagne bottles and an occasional joint tucked inside a hand. Most of them act as though their fathers own the place. Maybe one of them does.

David and I are technically not supposed to be here. It's a tradition for seniors; most of the juniors and younger dates usually go home or spend the night at someone's house. We're only going to hang out for a while and then catch a taxi back to get David's car. The plan is to watch the sunrise from the roof of his house.

People head up to the rooftop pool, but we escape to a borrowed suite. We slow dance and eat strawberries. It's the best part of the whole night for me, until the door flies open and three boys and a girl burst in with a camera, a script, and a tripod. They're doing a movie version of the musical *Rent* with a Baz Luhrmann twist, and the director, Micah, wants to shoot "Will

You Light My Candle?" in our room. I think they're all a bit crazy, but they're so hyper they make us laugh. They start rearranging the hotel furniture. David grabs strawberries, the champagne bottle, and me. We lock ourselves in the bedroom.

We kiss as we dance some more. After what seems like forever, the noise from the living room subsides and we're alone again.

"Thank God," David says. "I thought they'd never leave."

I look at him and tingle all over. Seriously.

"Did I tell you this evening how beautiful you are?"

"Only once."

"You are the *most* beautiful." He kisses me. "You know I'm madly in love with you?"

"I do. I love you, too."

"You know I really want to be with you."

"Yeah."

"It doesn't have to be now . . ."

"But it can."

Silence.

"Are you sure, Katie? Because nothing changes if we don't."

I can only nod. *In acting, we call it a beat. One part of the action is over and the next part begins.*

We dance so close I can hardly stand it. He reaches behind me for the zipper and my skirt drops to the floor. I put my arms up and he slips off my top. I'm standing in a thong and heels and every cell I own is glowing.

"Oh my God, Katie," he whispers. "You *are* the most beautiful." He pulls me gently toward him and we continue to sway back and forth. He kisses my neck and slowly runs his hand up and down my back. "I love you so much." He sighs.

"I love you, too." The feeling is so amazingly intense I can hardly stand up.

"Shall we?"

I nod.

"Are you sure, Katie?"

"I am so sure."

He leads me over toward the bed and slowly takes off his clothes—all the while saying how much he loves me, how beautiful I am, how much he's waited for this moment. I can hardly breathe. We lie down facing each, a foot or so apart. He kisses me, he touches me, we smile at each other. There's no hurry, no pressure.

This is exactly how a first time should be.

He traces the outline of my lips with his finger and travels down my neck to my chest. "You're perfect," he whispers. His arms go around me and he draws me close. I feel his breath on my neck. He starts to move in rhythm, slowly, gently.

Suddenly I'm terrified. Scared to death.

I remind myself this is what *I* want to do.

It doesn't help; my fear's a volcano erupting.

I tell myself this is right, this is good, this is how people act when they love each other.

My body is turning to stone.

I am shutting down; no amount of needing to stay seems to help. David continues to stroke me and kiss me, whispering how much he loves me. I'm terrified. I want to be done with it.

I thought knowing what happened would make it go away.

I was very wrong.

Somehow I manage to keep still. His hands are all over me, but I can't tell what he's doing, because I literally cannot feel it. I don't know if my body is responding because I'm no longer in it.

He loves me—I love him—He loves me—I love him. . . .

It's my prayer so he won't realize I'm freaking out, a mantra to keep me calm so he can finish. Then maybe I'll be normal again and the next time *it will be all right*. I don't know how much time passes before he says my name—in passion?

I love him—He loves me. . . .

"Katie." He says it again, louder.

My eyes open. He's pulled back away from me. His voice is flat and angry. "What's going on with you?"

I try to smile, but it doesn't work. "What do you mean?"

"Just what I said, what's going on?" He has never sounded like this.

I search his eyes for our connection; I can't find it. I'm suddenly conscious of being naked.

"You're not even here." He's disgusted, I can tell. "I'm holding a corpse."

I try to respond, but since I can't think and I can't feel, I sure as hell can't talk. I'm a lump, null and void.

"You have to talk to me, Katie. Otherwise I don't know what to do."

He waits; I watch him. I pray for words to explain, but my brain is a beehive and nothing is making sense. He's up now and starting to put on his clothes. His tone of voice makes me wish I could just disappear. "We didn't have to do this. I asked you. It would have been fine to just dance or do Micah's movie, or not even come here." His face is completely blank. I pull the pillow in front of me. "I thought we were, that you and I . . . Oh shit, I don't know what I thought." He's half dressed and he pauses to look at me. "You say you love me. You say you want to be with me, and then . . . you act like I'm hurting you or something. What is it? What am I doing wrong? Are you playing me? What?"

He throws his hands up, like I'm hopeless.

Which I am.

"Talk to me, Katie." It's a warning.

I want to. I want to tell him I love him, that right now I don't know what to do either, that I hope he'll forgive me.

But lumps don't talk.

Instead, I stare. I can't even shake my head.

"Okay. Whatever." He picks up my skirt and top and tosses them at me. "I'll be back in a while." He grabs his shirt and heads for the living room. A few seconds later I hear the door to the hallway open and close.

I don't move for a few minutes because nothing is processing. Finally I remember David said he's coming back and I need to be ready. I can manage that. I'm good at doing what I'm supposed to. I put on my clothes, fix my makeup, get my hair back up to a reasonable facsimile of before. I find my shoes and walk to the living room and sit down to wait.

When he comes back, I can't look at him, but I feel his stare.

"Okay, let's get you home." His voice doesn't know me; he's speaking politely to a stranger.

"Okay." We're silent as we walk down the hall. He kids with Micah and crew filming in the hallway, as if I'm not even there. We ride down in the elevator and trek across the hotel lobby and out to the front. The sky's still dark. He beckons to the first yellow cab parked in the turnaround. He holds the back door for me, then goes around and gets in the other side.

"It's all right," I manage to blurt. "I can—"

"I'm not letting you ride home by yourself."

He tells the driver where I live; we lapse back to silence. He walks me to the front door and before I can get the key out, mumbles, "Good night," and heads back to the cab.

THIRTY-ONE

He doesn't call Sunday. He does send an e-mail Sunday night saying he's going in late Monday morning and can't drive me to school. Michael takes me. He asks about Prom and I say it was fine. He pretends to believe me.

I look for David all morning. I don't see him. I don't know how one hour manages to pass into the next. I pretend to be a girl getting ready for finals. I pretend to listen to teachers, take copious notes, and engage in improvs in acting class; I even pretend to have a long conversation with Layla, who's going to Brown next year and wants to tell anyone who'll stand still long enough. She doesn't notice I'm pretending. No one does. Or maybe they do, and don't really care.

David finally appears, at lunchtime. He's across the alley, with Micah and Christina; they're all talking at once and laughing like crazy. I wonder if he's telling them about me. I wave. Either he doesn't see me, or he doesn't want to. He keeps laughing and talking. I duck into the greenroom for the rest of lunch. I don't see him after school. I have to call Michael to come pick me up.

Nightmares are supposed to fade when you wake up, but this one loops endlessly, threading itself through nighttime dreams and daylight hours. It has nothing to do with Monster fathers and their children; it's a close-up replay of the end of Prom night. Michael takes me to school all that week. David has a study group he's meeting with first period. We talk, briefly, or he does—at snack, but only to say we'll have to "really talk" after finals are over. I don't believe him.

Those whiny oldies I always laughed at now seem to make a great deal of sense. Hearts *do* break, or something does—otherwise I wouldn't hurt this bad. I start hiding out in the greenroom every day at lunch, hoping that not seeing him at all will make it easier. It doesn't.

Tess doesn't question me until Thursday. "Okay, baby," she calls from her office. "What's going on?"

"Nothing, just studying," I call from the couch. I toy with the idea of escaping to the alley, but Tess appears in the doorway.

"Where's David these days?"

"I don't know."

"Uh-oh. You guys break up?"

"I guess."

"Want to talk about it?"

I shrug. It's my new thing. I've finally managed to stop smiling. Shrugging shows intelligence *and* indifference.

She plops on the other end of the couch and crosses her legs. "What happened?"

I look into those young-old eyes, and the story trickles out, backward. I tell her about Prom night, and then San Francisco, and suddenly, I'm explaining the nightmares and the weird hallucinations—everything, from the ninth grade on. I can't seem to stop myself. She listens carefully and doesn't interrupt. About the time I get to the part about my dad, the bell rings and lunch is over. I reach for my backpack, but Tess beckons me into her office.

"No, no. Stay a bit; I'll write you a note," she says, closing the door behind us. "Now go on, please." She sits down behind her desk.

I'm beginning to have second thoughts anyway, and when I remember what happened with Stacey, I panic.

"If I tell you about someone hurting me, will you have to, you know, report it?"

"Is it going on now?" she asks.

"No."

"Are you sure?"

"Yes. It was a very long time ago."

"Then I do not."

And so I explain what I suspect about my dad. She moves from behind the desk and sits on the floor opposite me. She gathers her thoughts the way she does before she critiques a scene in class.

"Katie, have you ever heard of post-traumatic stress disorder?" she asks.

"What soldiers get?"

"Yes. And abused children."

"Oh."

"It could be what's happening to you."

"But I don't know for sure—"

"Well, let's think about it. It seems to me your nightmares and the way you end up feeling with David have a lot in common."

"I guess."

"So, maybe your mind is having trouble with this, but your body remembers, and so when David—"

The conversation has now gone too far. "You know what?" I interrupt. "I better go to class."

"Katie, this isn't your fault. Something scared you and you

had to shut it away. That's all."

"I have to go."

"I need you to listen."

"I don't want to. I don't want to talk about it anymore. I'm sorry I said anything."

"It might not be a choice. If you don't look at it, you're going to go right back to where you were."

"I don't care."

"Katie, for whatever reason, you're strong enough now to deal with this. You just have to remember it."

"I did."

"Yes, you did. You started to. You might need some help to go further."

This stops me. "You mean a shrink?"

"Yes, or a counselor."

"No. No way. I do not want to do that."

"Then maybe you should talk to your mom."

"I don't think so."

"Your brother?"

I stand. "Tess. I'm really sorry, I shouldn't have said anything. I'm fine, okay? And I really need to go."

"This isn't the sort of thing that will disappear all by itself." She reaches for the candy jar on her desk, hands me a Hershey's Kiss, and starts to open one for herself. "You saw that, with David, at Prom."

That's good for a whole new surge of pain, like touching an electric wire. "Yeah."

"If you can address the past, you can start thinking about talking to David."

"Like that would do any good."

"You might be surprised. He's a pretty exceptional human being."

"He's not always what you think, you know," I blurt, thinking of how he plays my mom and Tess, too. I sound angrier than I feel.

"Well, maybe not, but then, who is?"

"Anyway, he's done with me, that's for sure."

"You don't know that."

"I know he's ignoring me."

"Maybe he doesn't know what to say. Maybe he thinks you don't want to talk to him."

"But—"

"First things first. You need to look at the memories."

I meet her eyes and take a moment to explore. "You think they're real?"

"Absolutely."

"How can you be so sure?"

"Because little girls can't make up stories like that."

This stops me for a second. "Maybe I got confused."

"Or maybe your father did."

"I don't know, Tess. I just don't know. I can't believe he'd . . . I mean, I thought he loved me."

"I'm sure he did, Katie. Sometimes, it's two separate things."

Suddenly I'm glad Tess didn't let me run away. "I guess I could talk to my mom."

"I'll go with you, if you like."

"No, I have to do it myself. After the wedding. It's only like four weeks."

She shakes her head no. "I don't think you should wait that long. I think that's what your body's been trying to say."

THIRTY-TWO

Nothing is my beginning—and to nothing I return
Nothing feeds my soul and warms my nights
And as nothing is my life and my death
So nothing sustains me . . .
And I care for nothing
Just as nothing cares for me

I see nothing as clearly as sun-lined mountains
I feel nothing as the ocean on sand-warmed skin,
I tell nothing to someones who come asking
Nothing is my truth
Nothing is my only reason
Nothing is me.
And I, of course, am Nothing.

I'm supposed to be studying for my World Civ exam, but I'm perched on my balcony, reading. All I'd wanted was to find the report I did last year on William Shakespeare. Instead, I run into this envelope stuffed with poems. No dates on them, but the handwriting is young, definitely elementary or middle school. I know they're mine, but I don't remember writing them. I read over the one I found before we moved:

> *July vanished without a trace.*
> *August is the sun,*
> *setting, swelling*
> *like a fat orange candle*
> *losing its shape on the horizon*
> *Now melting*
> *My father is disappearing and will not let me see his face.*

What the hell did I mean, "my father is disappearing . . . ?" I used to think it was about him dying; now I wonder.

Why can't I remember this?

Why can't I remember myself?

A ton of World Civ notes and our huge textbook are spread out on my bed, waiting; the final is first thing in the morning and it's already ten o'clock. I know I need at least a C and I wish I cared, but the political framework for Elizabethan drama doesn't exactly affect my life right now. I want to think about important things—about David and my father. I want to figure out my self. Poking back into the envelope, I take out one more poem.

> *These are the days I walk between raindrops*
> *A shadow no eyes can see*
> *Reaching out*
> *but finding nothing*
> *Please someone tell me what I'm supposed to be.*

If I could remember when I wrote these, where I was sitting, what pushed me there—if I could remember being little—

maybe the puzzle wouldn't be so scattered. I might be able to see my father's real face. And maybe even my own.

Two weeks since Prom; it only *seems* like two months. But who cares—I'm having way too much fun flunking. Oh, and sitting alone in my favorite spot in front of the library.

"Hey."

My heart stops. I look up. It's David, of course, because why would he say hello to me when I look good?

"Hey." *At least I sound intelligent. Oh wait, no I don't.*

"Any more finals today?"

"Nope. All done."

"Need a ride home?" He asks, then snorts. "Oh shit, no, I can't"—*Whoa, am I making him nervous?*—"I have trig."

"It's okay. Michael's picking me up." *My heart is now pounding so fast I think he must be able to see it.*

"Oh. Good. Sorry about the rides and stuff. Finals . . . well, they suck, and college aps are next year, and . . . yeah."

"Yeah." *Why is he talking to me?*

"So you're all done?" He sits down, not too close.

"Mm-hmm. You?"

"Just the trig. But then I'm done."

"Good." *Wow, even more intelligence.*

"How'd you do?"

I have to laugh because I have no clue. "I could have passed. Or I could've flunked it all. I don't know."

"So, summer school, huh?"

"I guess I'll find out next week." *We're talking like we've never met.*

"Yeah. Hey, I was wondering if you maybe want to go to a movie or something this weekend."

"I can't. Sorry."

"Oh, no problem. I just thought I'd ask. It's okay." He stands.

"Well, anyway, I guess I better get ready for my—"

Heartbeat increases. Can you do cardiac arrest at fifteen? "David, it's not because I don't want to."

"Don't worry about it."

"My mom and I are going to stay out at the Malibu house, get it ready for the wedding reception." *Let it be known: I have no shame.*

"Oh. Okay."

"'Cause otherwise, I would." *None at all.*

"Oh yeah?"

"Yeah."

"Okay. Well, maybe we can do something during the week?"

"We're there until Thursday."

"Friday? Dinner, movie, walk around the mall . . . ?"

"Yeah. That'd be good."

Omigod. Is this happening?

THIRTY-THREE

"Did something bad happen to me?"

The second the words leave my lips I am catapulted into the Twilight Zone. I can't believe I'm doing this. I watch my mother's face carefully: something scary sneaks across it before a look of concern locks in.

"Like . . . ?" she asks. Robert inches away from her, maybe to give her a separate space or maybe because he saw the something too. She doesn't notice.

"Something with Daddy." *I haven't called him that in my head for ages now—why does it slip out?*

She blinks slowly, once and then again. I wonder if she wishes now she hadn't insisted that Robert be a part of this conversation. Her face swaps one feeling for another. The something flits past a second time and her tone moves one step away from sounding like my mom. "Are you asking if your father molested you?"

I don't like the word; it's miserable and dark.

I don't like my mother's face.

I nod.

"Why would you think that, Kaitlyn?" Accusing, as if I've done something. As if I made this up.

"*Something* happened, Mom." It's like being onstage and *hearing* your lines as they come out, sounding flat and fake. I wish now I'd taken Tess up on her offer.

I *almost* wish I'd never brought it up.

"That's ridiculous." Mom's voice isn't her own at all now; even Robert notices. It's shrill and traveling higher. I see him watching her more than he's watching me. "Your father would never hurt you."

"But he did." I steal a glance at Robert. There's no expression on his face.

"I don't know what to say. I can't believe I'm hearing this."

"He came into my room, when I was little."

"Fathers do that. I came into your room too. Do you think I molested you?" *If voices were weapons, I'd be bleeding from hers.*

"Bonnie." Robert's voice is calming.

"What?" She snaps at him, too.

"Listen to your daughter."

"Not if she's going to accuse me—"

"She's not accusing you. She's telling you that something happened to her. You need to listen."

"Fine." But it isn't, obviously. "Go on."

I call up Tess's face and remind myself of her words: little girls can't make this stuff up. I raise my head and meet Mom's stare straight on. "Something happened to me when I was six or seven. I don't remember exactly, but—"

She interrupts. "Then how the hell—"

"Bonnie. Shhh." Robert puts his hand on her arm. "Go on, Katie."

This makes my eyes tear. Of course. Never when people are being assholes.

I don't know what to call my father. I can't say "Daddy" now. "He came into my room at night. You and Michael were already sleeping. I don't *know* exactly what he did. But he scared me, a lot."

My mom is trying now to keep her voice under her control. "You're saying he did something . . . *sexual* to you?"

It's like a horror film; all the doors in the house slam shut and the good guy is sucked up backward through an endless dark tunnel. I drop my head again. I feel myself closing in, closing down. I can't help but hear the disgust in her voice; she spits out the words like she's ridding her body of a hair she's swallowed. And it's all directed at me. She thinks I'm the disgusting one.

Robert closes his hand around mine. My mother looks from me to him and back.

"I won't hear this." She storms out of the room.

Robert sits with me but it's quickly awkward, so he stands. "I'll talk to her," he says, oh so very gently. Then he stops at the doorway and looks back. "You've obviously given this a great deal of thought. Let your mom have a little time to catch up."

I nod and blink. No smiles now; it's past cover-up.

"You're very brave, honey."

Does that mean he believes me?

THIRTY-FOUR

What did people do before you could go online and find answers to secret problems? Oh right, they killed themselves.

Anyway, every site on mental health has plenty to say about the symptoms of post-traumatic stress disorder. It's a real thing. The traumatic event lodges itself under the conscious radar and is reexperienced by the victim time and time again, in disturbing dreams and possible hallucinations, often set off by external or internal cues that resemble the initial experience. Intense fear, a feeling of detachment from others, overwhelming helplessness, and disassociation from the environment are common.

If I'm understanding what I'm reading—and I think I am—Bingo, Bingo, and BIN-GO. Someone's scanned my secret self and analyzed me online. I read the whole thing several times and set Tess even higher on my very short list of the World's Most Incredible People. She nailed it. If she ever decides to give up the drama teacher thing, she could be a shrink.

I have to sit back a minute and let this settle in. I haven't been making it up. *I'm normal and connected, for real.* This is something

I have to understand and deal with, but there is no inherent flaw in my being. I'm just trying to survive. I'm doing it the best I can.

Other people go through this too.

That's a Big Sigh. I'm about to check out the "treatments" when I hear the old *ding ding ding* of an IM.

hamlet99 has sent you an instant message.
Do you wish to accept?

Do you have to ask??

hamlet99: hey
kt13: hey
hamlet99: how are you
kt13: gd u?
hamlet99: very good.
kt13: oh yeah? y?
hamlet99: i'm talking to you
kt13: o
hamlet99: i missed you

I think: *That must be why you ignored me for two weeks?* I say:

kt13: i missed you, too
hamlet99: did your finals go okay?
kt13: who knows? urs?

I wonder why we're having this conversation again.

hamlet99: i think i did pretty well
kt13: gd

hamlet99: so what have you been doing?

Dying inside, you?

    kt13: not much, u?
    hamlet99: thinking about us and prom

Uh-oh.

    kt13: o
    hamlet99: i went to see a medium
    kt13: about prom?
    hamlet99: lol no, not really, but sorta
    kt13: u got your fortune told?
    hamlet99: i got a past life reading

I am so confused.

    kt13: i'm confused
    hamlet99: yeah. hey, can I call you? This would be better in person

"Okay, this sounds weird when you say it," David says on the phone a few seconds later, "but it was totally awesome."

I don't care at this point; we're talking. "Okay."

"I never met this woman, all right? I just gave her my signature the day before the appointment, and she slept with it under her pillow." *He's right. It's weird.* "So, we're in this little room and she lights a candle and tells me I need to welcome the spirits when they come and then at the end, say thank you and goodbye, so they'll leave. Except I can't tell that the spirits are there until she starts talking."

"Why—did her voice get all creepy?"

"No, she starts saying things about me no one else should know. I swear. She looks like she's listening to someone I can't see and repeating their words. Then she starts talking about my soul, who it was in past lives and what it agreed to do in this lifetime."

"Like, promises you made?"

"Exactly. Except she calls them 'contracts,' and let me tell you, it's one thing to read about it and totally freaky to have it be about you."

"How do you know she's not making it all up?"

"Because everything made sense. Everything. All the things my soul wants to learn in this lifetime? It's what I feel. It's like I already knew all the stuff—I just didn't know I knew it."

"You are so losing me."

"Sorry, I guess you have to be there. But I do want to tell you the part about me and you."

"Me?"

"Yeah. She was talking about how the soul has to circle and explore and experience until it finds where it's supposed to be. And then it settles a bit; it fits more comfortably in the universe or whatever you want to call it, because it starts to be in the correct relationship with itself. Is this making sense?"

"Uh, that would be no."

He laughs a little. "You think I'm a lunatic?"

"Um, well . . . yeah."

"I wish you'd been there. It's much easier to get when you hear it from her."

"Go on, I'll try to keep up."

"All right. See—each soul travels through time with a group of other souls. So like, you may have been with your mom or dad in a past life, in a different relationship. You might have been the father, or you and your mom could have been brothers or sisters. And each time you come back, your soul agrees to experience something that will make you grow. Sometimes it works, and your soul settles and moves on. Sometimes it doesn't."

"I kinda get it. But how come she mentioned me? Was I your father or something?"

"No. At the end, she said I could ask questions, so we talked about you."

Whoa. Heart jumps, brain twirls, stomach flips.

"I told her your name, and she told me your soul is struggling to rearrange relationships so it can find a more solid place to be. It's circling—or maybe you're circling around it. I forget exactly. I figured it's probably about your dad."

Warning, warning. "What do you mean?"

"Well, when someone dies, all the other—"

"Wait a minute, hold it. How do you know my dad died?"

"Your mom told me a couple months ago."

All systems ice. "Why?"

"I don't know. I called and you weren't home, and we started talking."

"And all of a sudden she says, 'Oh, by the way . . .'?"

"No. No, it wasn't like that; she was talking about getting married or something—why? Didn't you want me to know?"

"I don't care. It's just weird, that's all." *More than you know.* "Neither one of you said anything to me."

"I'm sorry, I didn't think—"

"It's okay. No problem." *I wonder what else they talked about.* "So go on with your fortune lady."

"Okay, well, I told her your name—"

"We did this part."

"Right. Well, you and I have been together in the past, and

132

probably will again in the future. We could even be soul mates."

I don't say anything for a second, I'm still on my dad.

"Hello?" David says. "Are we still here?"

"Yeah. I was just thinking . . . that's pretty cool."

THIRTY-FIVE

Mom and I are in the living room of Robert's Mini Mansion, aka Bob's Beach House, folding napkins and making table ornaments for the guests at Mom and Robert's upcoming wedding. We aren't talking. That is, until she blurts, "Your father went through a really difficult time before he got sick."

I am seriously not in the mood for conversation about my father, unless she wants to explain why she and David have conversations about him. She is definitely off the Trusted Parent List, leaving only . . . oh. Yeah. That would be no one. But I have no bitterness. I don't feel left out at all, even though he's *my* boyfriend and she's *my* mother. I'm the Good Daughter. I'll be polite and listen.

"He lost his job. Just after he got the promotion he'd been working for. The company downsized. It was pretty over-whelming."

I think, *"Who* are *you?"*

I say, "Yeah, I can imagine."

She drones on. I nod and act like I'm paying attention. But I happen to know that I wouldn't even be here if it weren't for

Robert. I heard them "discussing" me—she didn't want me to come. Robert had to talk her into it.

That + (Talking to David) = (Screw You, Mom)

A formula! I did learn something in geometry!

"I had to get a job, and he stayed home with the two of you. That's when I worked at the college. Don't you remember?"

"Not really." *Can she not hear the boredom in my voice?*

"Well, you were only in first or second grade, I think."

"I actually don't remember a whole lot about any of my childhood, and—"

"I guess that's natural, huh?" She interrupts. *God forbid we talk about anything but her.* She finishes one of the table decorations and steps back to look at it. "Anyway, it was a hard time for him. Especially since I was providing the salary." She points to the finished decoration. "What do you think?"

That you're totally selfish?

"It's great, Mom. It fits the house."

"This place is something, isn't it?"

"Yeah. Sure is."

"Anyway, I just wanted to share that about your dad."

"Why?" *Uh-oh—direct hit.*

She pauses, and when she speaks again, her voice is somewhat deeper. "Mostly because Robert thinks I should."

"What do you think?" *Second volley.*

"I don't know what to think, Katie." I realize, as she turns to look at me, that it's the first time today we've made eye contact.

"This is really about what I told you, isn't it?"

"I don't believe what you told us, honey." That pushes her away again, and she looks to find a new decoration, even though the one she has in her hands isn't finished. "I mean, I don't think you'd lie, but I do think you made some kind of mistake. It doesn't make sense."

Whoa. Big one for her side. Initial impulses: *Tell her I'm pissed*

*about her secret conversations with David, say "Fuck off and die, Mom"
and walk away, or walk away without saying anything and never talk
to her again.*

Second thoughts: *Recognize what's happening to me, how I want
to disassociate (thank you, Internet search engine) and let Stupid Kate
take over. And—understand it's a* choice. *My choice.*

And so—I choose to stay.

I also choose *not* to speak.

She watches me a second and then goes on. Her voice
remains low and gentle. "Your father loved you, Kaitlyn. So
much. He loved both you kids."

I wait.

"He would never hurt you. He couldn't. He wasn't that kind
of man."

My lips tighten a little, but I still do not speak.

"Maybe you misinterpreted something. You know? Little kids
don't always understand what's going on, so they make up sce-
narios to explain it."

Ice is forming inside me at a spectacular pace. I have to phys-
ically move to keep myself from freezing completely. "I didn't
make it up, Mom."

She doesn't hear me. "I know you had nightmares. And he'd
go in sometimes to sit with you. Maybe you got confused, huh?
Maybe the nightmares folded over, and you thought he was the
bad guy or something."

"Did he close the door?"

"What?"

"Did he close my bedroom door?"

"When you had a nightmare?" She pauses to think. "I don't
think so; you didn't like that, remember? We always kept the
door open."

"Are you sure?"

"No, I'm not sure. I was usually asleep. He's the one who'd hear you."

"You didn't?"

"Hear you? No. But I sleep like a rock."

"That's not true, Mom. You woke up if I even walked down the hall."

"Well, Katie," she says, her voice defensive, "it wasn't the best time for me then, either, and the doctor gave me sleeping pills. So, no, I didn't always hear you call me."

"How about Michael? He was right next door."

"Yes, and pretty much living under his headphones, remember? A train could run through and he'd never know it."

My heart's doing a speed lap, but I'm working desperately to stay calm and keep my voice emotionless. It would be so easy right now to shut down and tell her she's right. Except then I'd be back where I was before.

She sighs, hugely. "Katie, I believe you think something happened to you. I just can't make the facts support that." Her voice is infinitely reasonable. It's a Mother Voice, and she's winning; I can feel it.

Nevertheless, I speak. "I don't remember having nightmares until much later. And then I called for *you*, not him."

"No, you had nightmares in kindergarten."

"How do you know, if you were taking sleeping pills?"

"Your father told me."

Yes!

Yes, yes, and *yes*!

I pause for the words to land. My voice gets even softer when I say, "So there you are."

Her voice is equally soft. "No, Kaitlyn. *No.* Your father would not have hurt you—ever—especially not like that. He couldn't. I knew him; I was married to him; he was not that kind of man."

Why won't she hear me?

"Besides, you would have told me. I know you would have. But you never said a thing." She speaks with conviction and a tinge of hurt. "*Never*, Katie. So it's very strange why now, all of a sudden, just when I'm getting married, you . . ."

"You must never tell Mommy, Skates. Never."

"He said you and Michael would go away."

"What?"

As I say the words, I hear the echo again; I know it's true. "He told me I was having a bad dream, and if I bothered you with it, you wouldn't want me anymore. You'd take Michael and you'd leave. That's why I didn't say anything."

In the silence that follows, I drink in the sound of the waves not fifty yards from where we sit. She shakes her head, as if jarring her thoughts will make them dissolve. I can't read her expression.

And right now, this minute, I don't care.

She picks up a new decoration kit and heads toward the door. For a second she pauses and looks back at me.

"If he hurt you—if he did that . . ." She shakes her head again. I can't tell if she is talking to herself or to me. "I don't know if I can stand it."

It is truly remarkable how two relatively intelligent human beings can spend a day together and never mention the huge contentious polar bear lurking about the middle of the room. But we do. We talk of the wedding and the weather, dresses and the weather, the weather and the weather. After dinner we escape to separate spaces.

By midnight I'm wrapped in a blanket on the balcony of "my" room at the Mini Mansion. There's no man-made light on the beach or out in the ocean, nothing to outline where the water ends and the sky begins. A misty fog hides most of the stars—only the brightest manage to twinkle through. Waves rumble their approach and then crash, pounding down against the shore. The frothy whiteness of the breaking water glows eerily as the moonlight hits and outlines its ripples' journey up the coast.

So many voices in my head—Tess's, David's, Michael's, Robert's, my mother's. Stacey's, too, from her journal—how strange. I sit in silence, allowing them free range, accepting the bombardment, wishing somewhere in there, I could hear my father.

Did he love me?

I'm not sure.

Did he come into my room?

Yes.

I sigh and give my self to the ocean. It begins to order the anarchy inside. Over and over again, it gathers and strikes and flows; true to a rhythm I wish I could always hear.

THIRTY-SIX

"Do you remember where you got your nickname?"

Mom and I are having breakfast on the patio. We've already walked on the beach, rearranged the stuff in the kitchen so we know where to find everything, and called home to check in with Robert. We're been here four days and will stay through the weekend; each day the big white polar bear lumbers about, but never completely leaves the room. David's coming for dinner tonight, bringing a DVD we can watch on Robert's big screen. Michael's joining us Saturday to help move the heavy furniture.

I shake my head no and stuff my mouth with a huge strawberry. There's something luxurious about ocean air and fresh fruit. It almost makes me able to stand my mom.

"You couldn't have been more than three, because Mike was in kindergarten. Anyway, we went to the circus, out at the old Cow Palace. After the show, we were walking through the tent where they keep all the animals. Mike was scared of them, but not you—not a bit! Anyway, there was this baby elephant in one of the open stalls—"

"I remember this!" I interrupt. "I was petting him and you were taking a picture and he grabbed me."

"Yep. Wrapped his trunk around your arm and started pulling you in."

"Omigod, yes! I was so scared." *Crash, bang, I've landed in the midst of my history.*

"Your dad snatched you back. But Mike was completely beside himself. You remember how Daddy used to call you 'Kates'?"

"Yeah?"

"Well, Mike starts jumping all around, screaming at the top of his voice, in the middle of the tent, and even the security guys came running. He's saying 'Kates-Kates-Kates' and it starts sounding like 'Skates.' Anyway, we're holding on to you, and this skinny bald-headed police guy keeps trying to calm Mikey by telling him, 'Don't worry, little boy, we'll find those skates.'"

"Omigod."

"Yeah, it really got us laughing. That, and relief that you didn't get eaten by the elephant. Somehow, it stuck. Your dad and Mikey both started calling you Skates."

"Wow. That seems like a whole other life."

"It was." Mom sighs; this is as close as we've come all week to acknowledging the polar bear. "But this one's turning out okay."

"I guess it is."

"Do you like Robert?" she asks.

"I don't know him very well yet, but yeah. I do." I reach to pick out another big strawberry.

"Katie. . . ." The tone of her voice makes me snap my head over. "I'm sorry."

"About what?"

"I'm sorry I didn't know what was happening to you. I promise you, if I had—I would have stopped it."

Heart—go.

"I mean that."

Brain—open up and take this in.

"I don't understand it. I can't fathom why your father. . . ." She works her face to keep from crying. "Why he'd ever be . . . inappropriate." She has to stop a moment; her mouth is clenched tight and won't let the words out. She nods and she reaches her hand out toward me. "I'm sorry I didn't believe you. And I am so very sorry it happened at all."

As we cry and hold each other, this woman becomes my mother again, and the polar bear tiptoes softly out of the room.

THIRTY-SEVEN

By the time we finish our (cough, Chicken Helper) fettucine Alfredo dinner—which I cooked, thank you very much—I'm beginning to wonder whether Mom and David would even notice if I walked out. He's manipulating her like good-looking boys can with moms, and she's sucking it up. I'm seriously ready to bust him when she excuses herself and heads upstairs. Ten points for the Mother-unit. Twenty if she'd done it earlier.

David smiles and compliments my cooking, I smile and say thanks, but now that we're alone, we don't seem to have much to say to each other. Too bad Real Life can't unfold like scenes in a play, with exciting dialogue, recognizable subtext, and a definite action to play. We fumble our way through clearing the dishes and end up outdoors, walking down the beach. The sun hovers bright orange above the horizon.

"I love this time of night," David says in a low voice, sounding like a complete stranger.

Yeah. "Beautiful, isn't it?" *My voice is just as forced.* I send a smile in his direction and am jolted by the intensity of his stare.

We look away and walk in silence until he asks, "Want to sit for a while?"

We find a spot without kelp and hunker down as the sun starts to sink. He doesn't put his arm around me; he does scoot up close. The air's cooling but the sand is warm from the day. We're shoulder to shoulder as the sun sets . . . *"like a fat orange candle. . . ."*

Whoa.

Point Reyes—I was with Ginny's family—we were watching the sunset. I scribbled the poem on the back of the take-out menu we'd gotten from a tiny restaurant called Lew & Colleen's, where Ginny's mom was ordering food. Ginny was cuddling with her dad on a rock near where I perched, and I was jealous. I missed my daddy. He wasn't around me much these days—he preferred to hang out with Michael. Wow. Already, I'd folded up the real memories and concealed them from myself. I missed him; that's all I knew. And that's when I wrote the poem.

"Katie?"

I look toward David and stare blankly for a few seconds.

"Are you okay?"

"Yeah." *Take a breath. Be here, BE HERE.*

"Sure? You're looking a little spacey."

"No, I'm good." *I am. I'm here. I've remembered a poem.*

"I'm sorry I was such an asshole," he says.

"Excuse me?"

"At Prom. I was an asshole."

"Oh." I have to struggle a bit to catch up. "David, it wasn't just you."

"Uh, yeah. It kinda was."

"No."

"Are you going to let me say my speech or what?"

He sounds almost petulant. I nod and wait.

"Okay, this is what I think. I think when two people have a relationship, sometimes they understand each other, and sometimes they don't. Especially when it comes down to male or female. Make sense?"

"Uh, no."

"Okay, say like there's a 'male' role and a 'female' role—basic biology, you know—procreation and all that shit."

"The sex thing."

"Exactly. The sex thing. That's what happened! I wanted you and then you were naked and I wanted you more, but all of a sudden you got freaky and I . . . I knew I should have stopped, but I didn't, and I was an asshole."

I start to speak but he puts up his hand.

"No. Listen. I knew something was wrong and I pretended I didn't. Then I got pissed at myself and you and everything got messed up and nothing came out the way I meant. I don't know what I meant. I just know I love you and I would never hurt you. And I am really sorry I did."

I'm here, 100 percent, I understand what he's saying to me—and I think I just may let him take the blame, at least for now. "I love you, too, David."

"No shit?" He looks like a little boy who got forgiven for breaking Grandma's favorite lamp. I pull his head in to kiss him, and two big-footed Lab puppies choose that exact moment to land smack dab between us. We burst out laughing.

"Oh dear," this anorexic redhead in a workout suit hollers, "I am so sorry." She jogs toward us, dyed hair flying, leashes in hand—Stacey in thirty years. The puppies tumble all over, nipping ears and tails, licking whatever skin they find. We're in hysterics, the stomachache and tears kind, until a seagull flies low and the puppies are off again, chasing it down the beach as their owner chases them.

"You are a dog person," David announces as soon as we're able to calm down.

"Oh yes. Definitely, no two ways about it."

"You'd have to be, wouldn't you? Because I am."

"It's a soul thing."

"Exactly." This time the kiss happens and we cuddle after. "So, are we okay?" he asks.

"I don't know. Are we?"

"Uh . . . yeah, I think we are."

"Then, cool."

"But you do need to tell me what my mom said about my dad."

"Okay."

"Not now, but soon." *Way to go, Katie. Polar bears, begone.*

THIRTY-EIGHT

My brother gathers huge rounded stones from the cliffs to the north of us and makes a circle with them in the sand, ten feet or so from the high tide line. In the center he piles dried kelp and the bits of driftwood he's picked up.

"Michael, are you sure it's okay to light fires here? Because I saw a sign that—"

"Shhh." He goes back to his job. "I know what I'm doing, Skates. I was a Boy Scout, remember?"

"You were not."

"Well, I wanted to be. And that's almost as good." He grins his stupid-brother smile. "Besides, didn't you say you were cold?"

"Yeah, but—"

"Okay. Hello? I'm fixing that. Can we shut up a minute and let me do it?"

When the fire finally gets going—and yes, he uses matches and not the old rub-a-stick scout trick—I have to admit it's pretty much the perfect ending to an awesome Sunday. Casey and David have just left. Mom and Robert are upstairs. And me and the Bro, here, are in sync.

"It's all set," he tells me. "I'm going home the week they get back from Cabo. I told Mom and everything."

"Is she pissed?"

"Not a bit." He grins. "I think she's kinda relieved."

"Who can blame her?"

"Hey—are you implying I'm hard to live with?"

"No, I'm saying straight out you're still a butthead."

"That's better."

"And I'm gonna miss you, a lot."

"Yeah, I'm gonna miss you, too." He stirs the fire with a stick. "It's kinda funny, huh, just when we finally start getting to know each other."

"Yeah."

We have a Nice Sibling Moment here—which is actually not so rare these days. I find myself wondering what we were to each other in our past lives. If it's true souls travel together, we must have had at least three or four lifetimes together.

"Why did you tell me that time that our father liked me best?" *Okay, where did that come from?*

"Left turn at Idaho," Michael says with a little chuckle. "Didn't we have this conversation already?"

"You got someplace you have to be?"

He tosses a log on the fire and makes a face at me. "You could just see it in him, Skates; he watched you all the time. He took you places, he played ball with you—or at least he tried to—you were basically hopeless. Sports challenged. You couldn't catch it when he handed to you."

"Yeah, but he did the same stuff with you."

"Not because he wanted to. More like he had to, like Mom said or something."

I don't like the tone of his voice. "Michael . . ."

"Don't worry, it only really sucked the year I was getting punched out by Kyle and Paul. Third grade. I didn't know what to do, and Dad didn't seem to have time to tell me, even though he was laid off then. Remember that? How moody he got? Anyway, he sure made time to hang out with you."

The hair on the back of my neck starts to prickle.

Michael's mouth tightens. "It pissed me off."

"He went in my room?"

"You don't remember?"

"Did he shut the door?"

"Yeah, of course, that was the worst. He shoulda been in my room, hearing about my life, even if he was depressed. No offense, Skates, but you had Mom."

"Wait a minute—did you hear me talking to him?"

"Not a bit. I stuck my headphones on and pretended I didn't care. And then he got sick, and it didn't matter anyway."

I am so fully alert right now I hear butterflies. "Michael, he didn't get sick until I was in seventh grade."

"Nope. I was in fourth—you were in second."

"No, no. I remember the conversation Mom had with us— we were in the living room and she told us he had cancer. I was in seventh grade."

"I know exactly the time you're talking about, Skates, but that wasn't the conversation. She was telling us he might not make it; that the chemo didn't work."

"I am so confused."

"You really don't remember this?"

"No."

"By then he'd been doing chemo for years."

"Really?"

"Yeah. He was diagnosed and went for a second opinion. He

had his lung removed, got radiation and chemo, and then he was okay for a while. But it showed up again. It all went on for years, Skates. I can't believe you didn't know this."

"I can't believe you didn't know what he did in my room."

"What do you mean?"

"Nothing. Never mind. Later. So, what else?"

"Well, okay, he had a couple of remissions, and we kept thinking it was going to be all right. But cancer cells kept showing up other places. Finally he just gave up."

"What do you mean—he gave up?"

Michael's mouth is twisted. "Just what I said. He gave up. This doctor had a whole new kind of drug he wanted to try, but Dad wouldn't do it."

"You sound mad, Michael."

"He could've tried it. It could have worked. We might not even be here now. But, oh well, huh. It was his choice and he couldn't handle it. So he quit."

"You *are* mad."

"That would be dumb, wouldn't it? He's dead."

"You still get to have feelings about him."

"Okay. Hold on. Stop. You are sounding way too much like a shrink. I'm really not into this conversation anyway, so let's either, you know, change the subject, or you go talk to Mom or David. Somebody who likes this kind of shit."

We bump sort of awkwardly around the house for the next few days. I feel like an actor who memorized the wrong script and didn't figure it out till the middle of act two. There I am, onstage, blustering through my lines, playing my actions, when suddenly I discover the back story isn't at all what I believed it to be. I don't recognize the other characters. I barely recognize myself.

Did Michael know why Dad was really in my room? Has he

buried the memory like I did? Questions and more questions—like who are you if you're not what you remember? If what you believed happened in your life wasn't true? Does that mean what I perceive now isn't real either?

I consider telling David everything. I also consider going back and confronting my brother—what did you really know? Why were you angry with me? And why are you running away now?

But something stops me, some unfamiliar little voice I don't recognize, arriving from outside my brain and interrupting my thought process. My soul speaking? I have no idea, and right now, I don't care. Circles and souls make as much sense as anything else.

THIRTY-NINE

It's weird enough to know your mom is getting married. But when you actually walk down the aisle as maid of honor, and your brother escorts her and gives her away—then you enter the land of Truly Frickin' Strange.

The ceremony's in a tiny glass-enclosed chapel not too far from Bob's Beach House, thrust over the ocean and framed on the mountainside by ancient eucalyptus trees. Not too many guests are invited—a girlfriend of Mom's, Steve and his parents. The few cousins left in Mom's family are people we barely know; invitations were sent, but only gifts arrived. Robert has several friends, but no family present, either; his daughters do not show up. I ask David, and Michael brings his new girlfriend, Paris.

I do the step-touch thing down the little aisle and stand over to one side. Robert enters from behind the altar as my mom appears in the doorway. Corny as it sounds, she glows. Outlined by the sky and the ocean, she stands posed like a ballet dancer as she takes Michael's arm; they float toward us.

I'm split in two: loving the absolute adoration on Robert's face when he looks at my mother and the little trace of tears in my mom's eyes, and obsessed with poring over my last conversation with Michael. All pieces of that same huge puzzle.

Two people preside over the ceremony. A white-haired woman priest with an incredibly gentle, melodious voice, talks about the vows that souls take in the sight of God. How two people come together and love each other so much they want their love witnessed by their family and friends. I sneak a peek at David—his eyes are glistening. I check Michael in his place opposite me—his eyes are shuttered.

In his turn, the male priest reads the vows that Mom and Robert wrote. They include the honor and cherish in sickness and health stuff, and a part about us—Robert's idea. The male priest reads it out loud; Robert repeats it to our mom.

"I promise to respect and to care for your children, Michael and Kaitlyn, to honor their lives, to show them all the love I am capable of giving, to shelter them whenever possible, and to try to have the wisdom to help them to grow."

Once again I find Michael; I want him to share in the tenderness and affection I'm feeling now for Robert, for Mom, and for him. He won't acknowledge me. The handsome young man who escorted his mother has morphed to a dark, melancholy boy. I want to freeze time, go and wrap my arms around him, and tell him everything's going to be all right.

Then it's done. We take every imaginable photo and head back to Bob's Beach House for the reception, where the caterers have spent the morning arranging things exactly the way Mom wants. David and I drive with "the wedding party" in an incredibly outrageous Rolls-Royce limo. David holds my hand like he'll never let it go and beams like a kid arriving at Disneyland. Michael's back in place again; I realize he wasn't remotely conscious of himself during the wedding. Paris slips her arm through his and snuggles close. He makes his "Oh shit, what do I do now" face, I start giggling, Mom glances over and beams at both of us.

Two hours later the celebration has settled. Robert's deep in conversation with one of his friends. Michael and David and Paris are arguing politics up on Michael's balcony, and my mom's standing by herself at the edge of the deck, just out of the sight of the party. I want to go sit with the ocean and ponder the day, but something draws me down to her.

"Hey you mommy," I say, softly, so I won't startle her.

"Hi, baby."

"You happy?"

"Yes. I am." She reaches over and takes my hand. "You?"

"Doing pretty good." I smile, she turns back out toward the water, with the same look I imagine I get on my face as the ocean calms me every night. Like mother, like daughter?

"Want to take a walk?" she asks.

"Sorry, can't, my mother said if I get the dress dirty —"

"What the hell does she know? Come on. Just keep it out of the—wait, shit, you know what? Get it wet. Go surfing. Catch a fish in it. I don't care. Come on. Let's walk."

We head up the beach in bare feet, hand in hand, holding up our skirts. We go all the way around the cliff that bulges out and into a little alcove where there's no house overlooking us. I imagine we must appear a tad strange in our fancy gowns, sitting on a sand bluff.

"Can I tell you something?" I ask, noticing how young she seems right now.

"Of course."

"I like your husband."

"Oh yeah?"

"Yeah. He's very cool."

"Well, I certainly think so."

"It's still kinda weird, though, isn't it? Being here, and every-thing."

She nods. "Very weird. But good."

"Yeah." I can feel us both relaxing as we listen to the waves. Then: The old Blurt Technique. "Mom, how long was Daddy sick?" *Will I ever leave well enough alone?*

"Four, five years, I guess. Why?"

"I thought it was only a couple of months."

"No, baby. Much longer."

"Why didn't I know that?" My voice is turning whiny.

"You were a little girl. You didn't need your whole childhood taken up with cancer."

"Michael knew. He's not that much older." *Shut up, Kaitlyn. Shut UP.*

"Michael didn't leave us much choice."

"It's still not fair." *Strike two. Why can't I leave this alone?*

"I'm sorry, honey. It seemed right at the time. I just wanted to protect you."

"I wish you had."

Strike three. We're both out.

How can I be so angry and not know it?

She starts to reply but checks herself. I can see her face work-ing not to cry, and I wish for Stupid Kate to appear. This Being Present thing sucks. I hurt people. I hurt myself. I spit out little barbs I don't even know I feel. I turned my mother's whole life upside down by remembering my father, and now I rub her face in it. On her wedding day.

I'm good.

"Mommy, I'm sorry." The words come out husky and low,

but I know she hears them. She doesn't move, except to gather in her shoulders. We're in tableau on the sand—is it going to be the opening scene or the final one? If she won't turn around—it's curtain, and I won't know what to do.

She sighs.

"Look what I'm doing," she mutters as she uses the hem of her dress to dab at the makeup streaks on her face. "This dress costs more than I do." We both smile. Then she stares straight into my eyes and suddenly, there's nothing else in the world except my mother and me.

"I don't know how to fix it, Katie."

"I know. Me, either."

"I would give my life to change what happened."

I can't find any words.

"I didn't know. I should have. But I didn't."

I manage a nod.

"I love you," she whispers. "You're my baby girl." One of those tears she was holding back finds its way down the side of her cheek.

"I love you, too."

She kisses my forehead, then puts Mom-arms around me and pulls me close. Stupid Kate waves as she exits. My mother and I sit watching the ocean, me wrapped inside her hug.

FORTY

I have the dream—running down the hallway, just as scared as ever, and the Monster's getting closer. He laughs as his slimy claws touch me and even though I know it's my dad—I also know it isn't—and I run faster, around the corner and straight toward an open window that's never been there before. I leap before I realize how high it is, but I'm okay, because I'm flying . . . except then I start to fall, tumbling over and over myself, screaming—until that strange little jerk happens that always wakes me up.

A second later someone taps at my door. "Katie? Is everything all right?" It's Robert.

I don't answer because I'm not quite awake. He opens the door slightly and peers in. I notice he's carrying a plate of sliced fruit. "You okay, honey?"

"Uh . . ." I sound spacey. "Yeah. I had a bad dream, I guess."

"I hate those."

"Me, too."

"Want a grape?" He holds the plate through the doorway, and for some reason it makes me laugh. He smiles back, pushing the door farther open, but staying inside the frame. "We leave in the morning. Mrs. Hoyt's sleeping over; she'll cook and drive you to school and stuff."

"Good. Thanks." It takes a second to remember Mrs. Hoyt is the housekeeper.

"And David's welcome to visit."

"Okay, cool."

"Not all night. Mrs. Hoyt *will* check."

I smile at him. "Got it."

"Good." He pops a piece of fruit in his mouth. I get the definite feeling he's hanging around to make sure I'm okay. "Well, I guess we're family now."

"Yep. I guess we are."

"I hope that's okay with you."

"Yeah, it is." Then it really hits me. He's my stepdad now, legally.

"All right then, I'm going to bed. Sleep well, now, and call if you need anything."

The next morning, "Dad" and I have breakfast on the porch while Mom packs. Michael's sleeping in. We watch the steady parade of locals out walking or jogging, including the anorexic redhead with the two puppies.

"So how are you doing with everything?" Robert asks, out of the blue.

"Okay, I guess."

He nods but doesn't say anything.

"I haven't had a lot of time to think about it."

"Would you like to talk to a therapist?" he asks.

"No, thanks."

"You realize you didn't do anything wrong?"

"Oh yeah. I've been reading up."

"Excellent, but I still think a therapist . . ."

I shake my head no. "I'm doing what I need to."

"Which is?"

"Remembering stuff, talking to Mom." I reach over for my water and take a sip. Robert's taking the dad-thing a little far. "My father didn't mean to hurt me. Something was wrong with him. He may even have been abused himself."

"It doesn't matter." Robert shakes his head.

"What?"

"It doesn't matter whether he 'meant' it or not. There's no excuse."

Brick wall. I can't talk for a minute. "But . . ."

"No buts, sweetheart."

"Robert, you're not hearing me. He loved me . . ."

"That's beside the point."

"You can't love someone and hurt them too," I argue, "not on purpose."

"Happens all the time."

I don't like where this is going. "Yeah, well, I don't think he knew what he was doing. I think he was very depressed, and—"

"Katie, Katie, you're not hearing me. *It doesn't matter.* He's your father. You're his child—end of story."

"I don't understand—"

"You understand more than you know. The part you don't get yet is what it means to be an adult."

I just stare at him.

"It's a basic truth, honey: He was the big person, you were the little one. Whatever happened in his life was never, *ever* reason enough to hurt you. He was supposed to keep you safe."

FORTY-ONE

"Katie?"

I turn at the sound, missing the edge of picnic table by inches, but *missing* it nevertheless. Layla and Stacey are coming out of the administration building. It's Layla who's spoken. "Omigod. Why are you here? It's summer," she says.

Stupid Kate volunteers, but the words are already out, sounding smooth and sure. "I flunked geometry, of course. What else? Why are *you* here? You guys graduated, remember?"

"My transcript got screwed up," Stacey explains, as if we always talk to each other. "I had to get a new one sent."

"Because we're going to Europe tomorrow," Layla offers. "With Jake and Henry."

"Henry?"

"He went to Brentwood," Stacey says.

Layla points to Stacey and smiles. "Big time Love thang."

"Oh yeah? Congratulations!" *Where the hell did that come from and why do I sound like they don't intimidate me anymore?*

"Thanks." A flash of the old bitchy Stacey flickers and all it does is make me remember her journal.

"We gotta go," Layla says. "You take care, Katie-katie."

I look over at David and smile. It's one of those incredibly delicious summer nights—nine o'clock and the sun is just now dipping into the horizon. Homework's done. We're walking down the beach. Mom and Robert are back at the Brentwood house, very happy and very married, and Michael's left for Santa Rosa. I've claimed the Mini Mansion, with Mrs. Hoyt, of course, and David comes every night for dinner. He brings his dog, Jesse.

"Why so quiet?" he asks.

"Thinking."

"Don't think so much."

I'm in love with David. Completely, totally, and not at all in the way adults seem to think teenagers fall in love. You don't have to be grown to know you've found the right person. He loves me the same. It is a miracle, and I totally know it.

"I'm thinking about what Carol said," I tell him. Carol is the medium David goes to see. She's also a "relationship therapist"— two birds, one stone—and I've met with her twice. Robert and Mom think it's great that I'm "dealing with things." They don't know we just talk about past lives.

"Want to tell?"

"Not yet. It kinda has to settle first."

"Got it." He takes my hand and kisses it. "Oh, guess who I saw at Starbucks?"

"No clue."

"Stacey and Layla. Stacey's going to Tisch, after they come back from France, of course."

"Good for her. She'll be away from the asshole." I'm not sure why I don't mention I saw them too.

Jesse comes bounding up the beach. He races in and out of the surf, and when he finally reaches us, he's sopping. Of course he jumps on me.

"I think I may just have to give him to you," David says. "He's obviously fallen in love."

"Yeah, well, can you blame him? Me—you—hardly a difficult choice."

"Oh yeah?"

"Yeah."

"So you think maybe he'd—"he scoops me up in his arms—"save you if I happened to toss you in?"

Kicking does no good—he's entirely too strong. "You wouldn't!" I scream obscenities, among other things, and he marches toward the water. Jesse trails happily behind.

"David!!!"

"You're going in!"

And I do—but I take him down with me. Jesse throws his sandy dog body into the surf right along side us, no doubt feeling like one lucky pup to have owners who know how to play.

Half hour later, we're changed and dry and sitting on the deck with hot chocolate. Mrs. Hoyt brought it out, wanting to make sure we know she's here. I cuddle with David on the swing and Jesse plops his huge self on top of us. It's like that day in rehearsal when everything fit. There's nothing I have to do but be here.

I feel more than hear David take a long, slow breath. Jesse echoes. We both laugh. A few minutes later he checks his watch. "Time," he murmurs.

"Yeah."

"Hey, maybe I should stay a little bit longer, huh? Mrs. Hoyt'll be in bed soon, and . . ." He looks like such a puppy himself right now, I can hardly stand it. I tilt my head to one side, but don't say a word. "Okay, okay, got it. But Jesse stays."

"Yes sir."

"It's a damn good thing you're so fucking beautiful."

"See you tomorrow, baby."

FORTY-TWO

Midnight, and a full moon. It shines down from the sky and up from the ocean at the same time. All the stars are visible—no fog cover at all. I creep past Mrs. Hoyt's room, chuckle at her snoring, and venture out onto the sand to sit huddled in the breeze, facing the water. Jesse snuggles down next to me. An entire country is behind us; this makes me smile.

I don't stay on the balcony anymore, or even the deck. I like to be close to the ocean, on the sand. It's a radically different perspective from here, watching the waves gather themselves and surge forward, pounding, then end in a swirl of froth, sometimes inches in front of me. It's an exquisite place to cuddle with a big warm dog, think about life and death and souls circling.

That little voice whispers:

Circle the soul softly . . .

. . . and a photo that used to hang in the hallway in the blue and white house slips into my head. I'm five and a half, on my way out the door for my first day of kindergarten. I'm bundled up in a sweater and jeans, holding a brand-new Snoopy lunch box, which is almost bigger

than I am. I smile as I see me, so young and so perfect and precise. And tiny. Very tiny.

But I like being little. I'm skinny, too, with gaps in my teeth and long thick hair pulled back tight from my face, braided. When I smile I tip my chin down a bit and peer up from under lashes that I curl with a dab of spit on my finger, absently and endlessly, sitting in the backseat of the car on the way to school.

I like to wait and find out how a place will be or what the other kids are doing before I jump in—then I'm fearless. I'm the one who'll jump over the creek in the back field behind my house. Who can climb higher in the old oak than Michael, and he's almost seven. I love my dog, Jonti. I love my brother, too, even though he ignores me at school just because I'm in kindergarten. When I get my feelings hurt, which happens a lot, I sit in the corner of the laundry room and Jonti crawls on my lap and I cry. Then I'm better.

The best day ever is when one of the first graders says I can play spy plane with them. Only me. Heart pounding and my cheeks flushing red, I follow him to "Spy Port" under the willow in the back of the yard. He puts me in the formation with the other first graders, and the five of us fly down the yard with arms flung backward. I can keep up! The joy of it is almost too much to bear. I feel the power of myself. I am important and amazing and I know for sure I can do anything.

My life is good. I have a best friend named Ginny. Even though Michael teases me, he doesn't do it mean like my next-door neighbor does. Once he even stuck up for me at school, when Maria Modine tried to push me down. I like our blue and white house, especially the willow tree on the side. I like watching my mom pour pancake batter into letters first, then filling in the edges of the circle so I eat a big K in a wheel. I like sitting on my daddy's lap when we're watching TV at night. I like the way he smells like Old Spice and cigarettes, and how he tickles me and makes funny faces. I don't even mind that his face is scratchy. When I'm with him, nothing in the world can hurt me.

Except—he does. He hurts me.
He creeps into my bed and changes everything.
He crushes my power and my importance.
He gives me secrets I can't even tell myself.
He steals my freedom and my trust.
He makes me disappear.

Jesse whimpers quietly and snuggles closer. He knows. With arms wrapped tight around my knees, I rock gently back and forth and watch as the tide comes in and the ocean finally reaches my feet. I don't actually feel it, though I think it must be cold. I'm numb with an understanding I can't fully describe. I'm remembering how it was to be small and helpless and hurt by the one person in the entire world who would never hurt you.

I'm remembering how it felt to disappear.

Robert is right.

There is a big person. There is a little one. And there is an order to that, which is sacred. The adult takes care of the child. *The roles may not be reversed.*

He's my father.

He was supposed to take care of me.

I'm his child.

There are boundaries that should never be crossed.

AND NOW

Crying wears me out. But each time I slip down to the ocean and bring my little girl out, I do it. For hours.

I think: I'm in mourning. Again. This time it's not for my father who died—but for the death of the man I thought he was.

And for the life of the little girl.

My "truths" have shifted. There's no final answer, no absolute right or wrong. There is an order that works—a relationship between souls that allows them to grow. But no one truth. Each soul seeks its own. I have to search for mine and the way it fits into my life now.

"And if you say everything has a purpose in the world—what is the use of pain?!" Tilda's words from my audition monologue drop into my head. I don't dismiss them; the universe speaks in many ways.

I won't stop loving my father.

One day I might stop hating him.

And in the meantime, I have to cry.

Sometimes the tears thrash about and tear at me like a wild

animal; I rage at my father and my mother and every single adult in my world then who didn't notice something very awful was happening.

Sometimes the wound seeps quietly and the pain is low and mean and relentless, and the tears that finally, barely, escape from my eyes and throat are pinpricks of release, and welcomed. This kind of crying is the worst.

Always I am tired after.

Always, strangely, I feel just a little more "right."

And life goes on.

Mom answers my questions the best she can and we both cry and hold on to each other and try to place our hurt. Michael calls every week and attempts to talk me into moving back to Santa Rosa. He misses me. Robert lets me know he's there and will provide for me. Carol explains how my soul is strong and capable and can handle whatever it has to—and I think one day I'll tell her about me and my dad. Probably after I tell David and maybe Michael. When I'm ready. But not yet.

I was alone in the bedroom in the blue and white house; I was alone with the memory I couldn't have for all those years; and that's what I need to be for now, alone, to figure me out.

That's the purpose of pain.

Each time the crying stops, another fragment of anger and hurt is sliced off the gigantic mass of ugly feelings I've collected and hidden all these years. It floats out and away and in that instant I sense what it will be like when I fit into my self—*like I did when I was five.*

Then, of course, I crash—back to Stupid Kate, knowing nothing; helpless and hurt and scared—just like my little girl. Except the door's no longer shut. And now there's David and Robert and Michael. And my mom.

So I can cry again.

Jesse doesn't like it. He whimpers his little dog sounds and nudges my hand with his nose. He wants me to smile, so I do. I hug him and he burrows under my arm and lays his big head on my lap and relaxes. He's fine then, because he feels connected. I'm starting to feel connected too, to David, to my mom and brother, to the world. My soul shifts, and I circle it softly.

I try to stay here, in this moment. I try to breathe. And listen. And just *be* . . . my self. It's really all anyone has to do. It's very simple.

Oh wait . . .